INTO THE JAWS OF DEATH

As they ran across the Golden Gate Bridge, a bullet *spanged* off a girder. Frank looked over his shoulder. Feodor and Oleg were out of the car, shooting at them.

"We'll never make it," he said.

Joe eyed the dark waters below. "There's one chance," he said.

"Too dangerous," Frank said. "If we get caught in the undertow—" He cut himself off as he glanced over his shoulder, then back at Joe. Feodor was down on one knee, taking careful aim.

"Right," said Joe. He knew that look in his brother's eye, the look that said one chance in a million was better than no chance at all.

"Let's do it."

THE HARDY BOYS CASEFILES™ NO. 6

GREY CASTLE PRESS

Library edition:
GARETH STEVENS PUBLISHING

First Grey Castle Edition, Lakeville, Connecticut, September, 1988

Published in Large Print by arrangement with Simon & Schuster, Inc.

Printed in the U.S.A.

Library of Congress Cataloging-in-Publication Data

Dixon, Franklin W.
   The crowning terror.

   (The Hardy boys casefiles ; no. 6)
   Summary: An attempt to help their kidnapped uncle leaves the Hardy Boys stranded in a strange city far from home, being hunted down by two desperate gangs.
   1. Large type books. [1. Mystery and detective stories. 2. Large type books] I. Title. II. Series: Dixon, Franklin W. Hardy boys casefiles ; no. 6.
[PZ7.D644Cs 1988]   [Fic]   88-22309
ISBN 0-942545-47-8 (lg. print)
ISBN 0-942545-57-5 (lib. bdg.: lg. print)

Chapter

1

"MR. HARDY!" THE headwaiter called. "Your table is ready for luncheon."

Frank Hardy blinked lazily, shaking his head to toss his brown hair away from his eyes. He had almost fallen asleep, sitting in the Club Kiev's waiting room.

"Finally," Frank's brother, Joe, who was seated beside him, said. Energized by the thought of food, Joe sprang to his feet. He stood six feet tall, and though Frank was an inch taller still, Joe's springy blond hair made him seem the same height. Joe was burlier than his brother and looked as if he could hit hard. A natural on the football field, he looked out of place in the Club Kiev.

Frank stood up, too, very aware of the glances from the other men waiting for tables. Those older gentlemen fit the restaurant's image perfectly. They blended in with the dim lighting and aging furniture. Frank and Joe were the youngest people in the room—by about forty years.

It was weird, Frank had to admit. Here he was in New York City, where an eighteen-year-old could find the most hip restaurants on earth. Instead, he was in the stodgy Club Kiev. He sighed. It hadn't been his choice. They moved toward the white-haired headwaiter, who stood next to the dining room. Nothing ever seemed to change at the club, not since it had opened in the 1920s. Its style and menu hadn't changed in all the intervening years, nor, seemingly, had its personnel. As Frank approached the headwaiter, he thought he caught a hint of disapproval in the old man's eye.

Teenagers were common in most restaurants in the city, but at the Club Kiev they clung to a long-dead past and found any change hard to tolerate. Teens had their place, but it was obvious the headwaiter believed that place was elsewhere.

"Good evening," Frank said in Russian, and the older man's face brightened.

"You speak my language?" the headwaiter asked.

"Not much and not well, I'm afraid," Frank replied. "But it's a beautiful language. I'm Mr. Hardy."

For a moment the headwaiter squinted with confusion. "Ah!" he said and smiled. "You are

Fenton Hardy's boy. You have his eyes. For you, we will make a perfect meal." He pulled two menus from his podium. "Lunch for two?"

"Three, actually," Frank said. "We're waiting for a family friend. I'm Frank, by the way, and this is my brother, Joe."

"Good, very good," the headwaiter said as he pushed into the dining room. The boys followed, crossing the brightly lit room until they reached a small booth on the side wall. The elderly Russian swept a hand over it, waving them in, and Frank and Joe slid along seats on opposite sides of the table. With a slight bow, the man handed them menus and before leaving, he asked, "You will be following in your father's footsteps?"

Joe glanced up, puzzled. "Excuse me?"

"As detectives," the headwaiter said. His eyes were wide with excitement. "Your father is a great detective. He saved this restaurant many years ago. It would be a shame if such greatness were not handed down."

Frank checked a grin. "We haven't decided"—the Russian's smile faded—"but we're considering it."

Pleased, the white-haired man nodded and turned away. As he looked across the room, he stiffened.

A man was strolling toward the booth, white curls spilling on his forehead and highlighting his dancing green eyes. Though well on in years, the man was lean beneath his business suit, and

3

anyone who hadn't seen his lined face and white hair might have mistaken him for someone of Frank's age.

"M-Mr. Hunt," the headwaiter stammered. "I'm sorry I wasn't at the door to greet you." It was evident from the smile on the other man's face that the Russian took the situation far more seriously than he did. "Let me find you a table."

"It's all right," Joe said. "He's with us. How are you doing, Uncle Hugh?"

"Just fine, Joe," Hugh Hunt replied, sliding into the booth next to Frank. He wasn't really their uncle, but only a good and older friend of Fenton Hardy's. When they were younger, the boys had begun calling him "uncle," and the name stuck.

They had never been sure of the exact connection between him and their father. They knew the two men had known each other in the army, but then they had moved in different directions. Fenton Hardy became a detective, and Hugh continued in the insurance business, eventually starting his own company, Transmutual Indemnity, and retiring just a couple of years before.

The two men had less and less in common as they grew older, but Hugh was always there for the Hardys. Fenton Hardy never missed a chance to see him, sometimes even taking time off from a vital case to meet with him. It was something Frank and Joe accepted but never really understood.

"I'm sorry your father couldn't be here," Hugh said.

"Dad's in England with Mom and Aunt Gertrude," Frank said. "He told us to extend his apologies, but Mom's been bugging him to take a vacation for a long time, and his schedule finally opened up, and . . . well—"

"I understand perfectly," Hugh said with a wink. He flipped open the menu and ran his finger down the listings. "They have a great borscht here, if you like beets. For a main course, the chicken Kiev is—" He squeezed the fingertips of his right hand together, pressed them to his lips, and kissed them with a loud smacking sound. "There's nothing better than great Russian food, and nowhere is it better than here."

A waiter appeared at the end of the table. In a thick Russian accent, he asked, "Would you like anything to drink before your meal?"

"A round of your best Russian tea," Hugh replied, looking at the boys for their approval.

"None for me, thanks," said Joe. As much as he liked his uncle Hugh, the man's tendency to make decisions for everyone always annoyed him a little. Joe's small acts of rebellion helped keep the peace between them, gently reminding Hugh that not everyone shared his tastes. Curiously, Frank never contradicted his uncle.

When the waiter had left, Joe said, "You're looking good, Uncle Hugh."

Blushing, the older man flexed his arm so the

bicep bulged beneath his jacket. "You mean this? Keeps my insurance rates down. You look in great shape, too. What have you two been doing with yourselves?"

Joe inhaled deeply, weighing his answer. What could they tell him? That Joe's girlfriend, Iola Morton, had been killed by a mad terrorist group called the Assassins, and as a result the boys had decided to devote themselves to bringing dangerous criminals to justice? "Oh, you know. We go to school, and still help out our dad on his cases—"

"Actually," Frank cut in, "we don't spend that much time in Bayport anymore. Most of the time we're fighting supercriminals and terrorist organizations. So we spend a lot of time traveling. We get help sometimes from a government agency called the Network, but they don't really like independents like us getting in their way. All in all it's interesting work."

Joe's jaw dropped. Their parents didn't even know what Frank had just revealed to their uncle Hugh. He couldn't believe, after all they had done to keep their work secret, that Frank had just blown it.

Hugh stared at Frank for a long moment, studying the boy's face. Finally, a smile crept along his lips, widening into a grin until Hugh burst into laughter.

"Sounds like you need a good insurance policy," Hugh sputtered between laughs. "That's a good one, Frank. You're developing quite a sense of humor in your old age.''

Frank began laughing with his uncle, and Joe giggled nervously. Hugh didn't believe Frank. Joe realized then what Frank had known all along, and Joe felt a rush of new respect for his brother. It was a gambit worthy of Joe himself.

The waiter reappeared with two heavy white cups and a china teapot on a tray. He poured a cup and set it in front of Hugh, and then poured one for Frank. The spicy steam rose off the cup and wafted into Joe's nostrils, and he wished he had ordered tea after all.

"So what have you been doing lately, Uncle Hugh?" Joe asked.

"Oh, this and that," Hugh said, lifting the cup to his lips. "I do a little freelance insurance advising now and then." He closed his eyes and drained the cup, and with a look of satisfaction, he set it back into its saucer. Glancing down, he began, "You should become a tea drinker, Joe. You don't know what you're mi—"

He stopped suddenly, and his face went a sickly white. His eyes locked on the cup. "Where's that waiter?"

"He went back to the kitchen," Frank said. "Why?" He received no answer. Without another word, Hugh scrambled from the booth and dashed toward the kitchen. "Joe, go after him," Frank ordered.

Nodding, Joe followed his uncle, who had already disappeared through the swinging steel doors to the kitchen. Frank picked up the teacup and looked into it. At the bottom of the cup were black indelible marks. Cyrillic, Frank realized with a start. Letters in the Russian alphabet.

Anxiously, the Russian headwaiter appeared. "You are not pleased with the service?" he asked.

"You read Russian," Frank said and thrust the teacup at him. "What does this say?"

Puzzled, the older man took the cup and squinted at the letters. His mouth fell open in horror, and his eyes bulged. "No! No!" he shouted, hurling the cup to the ground.

"What is it?" Frank demanded.

Trembling, the headwaiter replied, "It says, 'You have just been poisoned.' "

Chapter

2

JOE CRASHED THROUGH the swinging doors. It looked like an ordinary restaurant kitchen, all sleek, bright chrome to contrast with the dark wood of the restaurant itself. The dozen chefs, waiters, and busboys spun to look at him and all motion froze for a second. Not surprising—he had just invaded their territory. But it didn't explain the fear in their eyes.

And suddenly they were moving again, ducking to the floor and scrambling for cover among the stoves and cabinets. Then Joe saw what they were running from. At the far end of the kitchen, next to a closed fire door, two men dressed in black suits had Joe's uncle Hugh by the arms and were forcing him toward the door.

The taller of the men had a dark beard, and a black patch covered his left eye. In his hand he held a Mauser with a silencer screwed on to the end of its barrel.

The gun made a sound like two cupped hands clapping gently together, and Joe hurled himself to the floor as the shot spattered against the swinging steel door behind him. It was the silencer that had saved him, he knew. At a distance of a few feet a gun with a silencer meant instant death, but over several yards a silencer would throw off the bullet's trajectory. For Joe, that fraction of an inch had been the difference between life and death.

"Joe!" he heard his uncle Hugh shout. "Get out of here!" Joe popped his head up over a counter to see the shorter man clamp a black-gloved hand over his uncle's mouth. A bullet *spanged* across the chrome counter near Joe's ear, and he ducked back down.

He rolled across the floor, trying to figure the odds against him. It was at least forty feet to the back door, and he realized there was no way he could get there, moving on hands and knees, before the men in black forced his uncle out the door and got away.

Let Frank worry about odds, Joe decided. Keeping low, he dashed past a line of counters and rounded a refrigerator. On each side of him, the restaurant employees were cringing, not believing that he would keep heading for the murderous pair. Joe turned the corner of an oven, where the smell of searing meat choked him. How far? he wondered. Were they still there?

At first he saw only a foot in his way. Cautiously he looked up, and above him stood the bearded man, his lips parted by a cruel smile. He said something that Joe didn't understand, but the motion of the gun made the meaning clear. Up it jerked, ordering him to his feet. Joe considered rushing the guy. But he knew the bearded man would have a clear shot at him. And this time, Joe knew, the silencer wouldn't alter the bullet's path. Joe stood up, hands raised to shoulder height.

No one else in the kitchen moved. The bearded man's smile widened as he pressed the tip of the gun barrel to Joe's forehead. Joe's breath caught in his throat as the bearded man chuckled softly and slowly began to squeeze the trigger.

With a muffled cry, Hugh bit into the gloved hand covering his mouth. The shorter man shrieked in pain and loosened his grip on Hugh. The bearded man turned slightly to see what was wrong.

That was when Joe swung his fist up, knocking the bearded man's arm aside. The gun went off, and the bullet lodged harmlessly in the ceiling. The man recovered instantly and jabbed out, clipping Joe on the chin with the gun butt.

Joe fell back in a haze of pain. Across the room his uncle Hugh struggled with the shorter man, who called to his companion for help. Ignoring Joe, the bearded man sprinted over and planted a fist in Hugh's stomach. As Hugh doubled over, the shorter man slammed him against the door. It opened, and the three of them vanished through it.

"Joe?" asked Frank Hardy as he pushed through the kitchen doors. "Where's Uncle Hugh?"

"In big trouble, I think!" Joe shouted. He dashed for the back door. "Two men just dragged him out this way."

"There's a narrow passageway behind the club," Frank said. "It spills directly out onto Fifty-third Street. Try to catch up to them. I'll head out front and we should have them surrounded." Without another word, Frank darted back through the swinging doors.

Joe reached the passageway in time to hear the roar of a car engine on Fifty-third Street. He saw his uncle and the bearded man seated close together in the backseat of a gray sedan. The shorter man sat in the driver's seat.

Sliding down the window, the bearded man snapped off another shot at Joe. Brick chips stung Joe's face as he ducked back into the doorway.

The car pulled out into the traffic. Joe looked up and saw his brother on the sidewalk just ahead. "Was that the car?" Frank shouted.

"Yes," Joe mumbled, barely loud enough for

Frank to hear. Joe was angry at himself because the car was gone, and their uncle was beyond help. Joe dusted himself off and ran out to join Frank.

"Hurry up!" Frank said urgently. "They'll get away." Already Frank was running after the car, leaving a bewildered Joe standing on the street corner.

Then Joe turned and saw the tail of the car, *just* turning the corner. Of course! he realized. This is Manhattan! If it were night, the car might possibly be able to speed off, but it was midday, and New York's streets were clogged with traffic. The Hardys had a better chance of moving quickly than the car did. Their uncle's kidnappers hadn't escaped after all!

The rush of excitement brought to Joe a surge of speed. He dashed along the street, quickly catching up with his brother. The sedan was half a block in front of them, but they were gaining on it with every step.

"You're the track star," Frank said to Joe. "Why don't you sprint up there and try to slow them down? I'll be right behind you."

Joe nodded and took off. He wanted another crack at that tall guy. In the restaurant he may have used a gun, but on the crowded streets a shot, no matter how quiet, would be noticed. The police would be called, and in that traffic, the kidnappers would have little chance to escape.

They would have to fight without guns, and once Joe got his hands on him, the bearded man would have no chance at all.

A honking erupted from the gray sedan as Joe neared it. The streetlight was green, and the sedan pushed vainly forward, struggling to get through the intersection before the light changed again to red. But traffic blocked the way. Only a few feet separated Joe from the car now. He stretched out an arm to open the back door.

As the traffic light switched to yellow, a gap appeared in the intersection. Joe's fingertips brushed the handle, but it was too late. The car lurched forward, then sped across the intersection as the light turned red, leaving Joe stranded in the middle of traffic.

Cars blocking him, Joe watched the sedan move farther and farther off. From the corner of his eye, he saw Frank trapped on the street corner behind him.

I'll just have to *make* a path and try to follow them, Joe decided. He took a deep breath, crossed his fingers, and lunged into the oncoming traffic. A taxi slammed on its brakes and skidded.

Joe twisted as he jumped. He slammed onto the cab's hood and rolled across the windshield, then slid down off the far side of the car, landing feet first on the pavement. Ignoring the cabbie's angry threats, he continued his pursuit of the sedan.

He could still see it, half a block ahead, stalled once again in traffic. Time seemed to stand still as

Joe drew nearer and nearer to the motionless car. He was dimly aware of the tall man turning his head in the sedan's rear window, his face filled with rage.

Joe grabbed the door handle, tearing the door open. The tall man's foot jabbed out, striking Joe in the stomach. The air *whooshed* out of him, and Joe fell back, smashing into another man.

As Joe tried to balance himself, he looked up into the newcomer's face. There was nothing recognizable about it, apart from sunglasses that covered his eyes. Like the others, the man wore a nondescript black suit, and his face was as expressionless as a mannequin's.

The kidnappers stepped out the far side of the car, dragging Hugh with them. Joe was on his feet, struggling to run in pursuit. But the man in black behind him clamped a strong hand on Joe's shoulder and stopped him.

"You've interfered enough," the stranger said coldly. "We'll handle this." At the snap of his fingers, some other men jumped from cars and took off after Hugh and his kidnappers.

"Get your hands off him!" ordered Frank, running up to them. Swiftly, the man in black reached inside his coat.

"Look out!" shouted Joe. "He has a gun!" He twisted from the man's grasp, ramming an elbow into his chest. With a sharp cry, Frank spun, aiming a high kick into the man's midsection. The man in black doubled over, his sunglasses flying from his face. He staggered back, whipping his hand from under his coat. It held, not a gun, but a small leather wallet.

He flipped it open, and Joe Hardy gasped. The wallet held a card that read: United States Espionage Resources. The man was a government agent!

"You're both under arrest," the man in black said.

Chapter

3

"So, you're the Hardy brothers," a hoarse voice said.

Frank and Joe had been sitting silently in the pitch-black room. They had remained in their chairs, uncertain of what might be waiting for them in the darkness. Their captors, Frank knew, would come to them soon enough.

At the click of the door opening, a soft blue light was diffused through the room. First they had heard the footsteps, and seconds later the man stepped in and spoke to them.

He was not the same man who had brought them in. This man was also dressed in black, but he was shorter and older, with curly black hair receding on both sides, leaving a widow's peak on his forehead. His small, dark eyes were burning, and his mouth was curled in a smirk. In one hand he held a file folder stuffed with papers.

"Let's not everyone speak all at once, okay?" the man said. "Frank and Joe Hardy. Quite the young adventurers, according to our reports."

"If we're under arrest, we want to speak to a lawyer," Frank said coldly.

The man leaned against a wall. "Oh, you're not under arrest," he said, shaking his head. "We only say that so people won't give us any trouble. By the way, my name's Starkey." He held a hand out to Frank, who didn't take it.

"Then we're free to go?" Joe asked.

Starkey chuckled. "Wake up and smell the coffee, chum. This is what you call protective custody. I've got a lot of questions about you that I'd like cleared up.

"Every time there's a spy or a crook running loose, you seem to be around. Some people might think you're more than a little involved in these situations. Like the one today, for instance. Is it just coincidence that you got in the way of my men, just when we were about to nab a master spy?"

"You're crazy," Joe said. "We're the good guys. We *stop* crooks and spies. Besides, whoever your 'master spy' is, he had just kidnapped our uncle Hugh."

"We don't have to tell him anything," Frank interrupted. "He's not the law."

"Maybe not," Starkey replied cheerfully. "But I sure am the government. So don't think I can't make plenty of trouble for you if you don't get cooperative real fast."

"If you're really a government agent, get in touch with the Gray Man at the Network," Frank said coldly. There was something in Starkey's manner that irritated him. "He'll vouch for us."

Starkey pinched his chin with his fingertips, as if pondering what Frank had said. "The Network. Frank, let me tell you what the Network means to me. Their budget and ours come from the same fund. As far as I'm concerned, all they do is leech money from Espionage Resources."

He gave the Hardys a nasty grin. "So nuts to them and their vouching. You haven't said anything to convince me you and your brother aren't spies, and until you do, don't bet on any help from the Network. They know I'd use any opportunity to convince the boys upstairs to take away their funding.

"All you and your brother are to the Gray Man right now is an embarrassment." Starkey squared his shoulders and continued. "Let's get back on track. Tell me what you know about Hugh Hunt."

"This is a joke, right?" Frank said. "My uncle Hugh and my father have known each other for years. He's in insurance. What's all this about?"

As if he hadn't heard, Starkey flipped through

the file. "According to the Network files, you boys are supposed to be pretty smart. Sounds to me like you're lying or you were born yesterday."

"I don't believe the Network would hand out files on us," Joe said.

Starkey laughed again. "All I had to do was tell them I caught two of their freelancers mixed up in an espionage ring and they practically rolled over and played dead. Everyone's twitchy about possible double agents these days." His smile suddenly vanished. "I honestly don't think you work for Hugh Hunt, though the evidence could easily be read that way."

"Work for him?" Joe asked, bewildered. "Do you really think we sell insurance?"

Starkey stared at him for a long moment. "You really *don't* know, do you?" The government man was almost laughing by then. "I probably shouldn't tell you anything, but if you're to be of any use to me, you'll have to know."

"Use?" asked Frank. "What are you talking about?"

"Don't you hate the light in here? I do," Starkey said, again ignoring Frank. He stretched an arm out, and with a click switched on an overhead light.

The room was small, about six feet by six feet. It was sparsely furnished with three plain wooden chairs and a small table. On the far wall was the door and a large two-way mirror. Frank couldn't tell if anyone was outside watching and listening or not. Starkey straddled one of the wooden chairs.

"That's better," Starkey said. "Now, let me tell you a little story about two men. We'll call them Fenton Hardy and Hugh Hunt, okay?"

"Don't you dare drag my dad into this!" Joe snapped.

Starkey raised his hands in mock surrender and shook his head. "I wouldn't dream of it. That is, unless you boys think there's some reason to." Both Frank and Joe glared silently at him. "Good. Now can I get on with my story?

"During a war in Southeast Asia, Hardy and Hunt met in the army. Now Hunt was quite a bit older than Hardy and already working for Military Intelligence. Hardy was recruited by Hunt and soon both were partnered, working for M.I. They were one hot team, I tell you, busting spies that no one else even guessed existed. You could base thrillers on these guys. Only they were under oath never to tell anyone about their actions."

"We know all this," Joe lied, hoping to shatter Starkey's smugness. But the man ignored him. "So what?"

"So when his hitch was up, Hardy returned to civilian life as a detective." Starkey leaned back. "Meanwhile, the boys upstairs asked Hunt to start up his own counterintelligence service, answerable only to us or the President. They were very convincing. Well, old Hunt's a patriot and not one to turn down an offer from Uncle Sam. So he starts up this spy firm—"

"No way that happened," Frank interjected. "Our uncle Hugh was in insurance."

"I really never thought you were a sucker, kid," Starkey said. "You think we have a sign out front saying United States Espionage Resources? Your uncle's insurance company was a front. Just like we all have fronts. To everyone else, we're just ordinary businessmen. That's why they call us *secret* agents."

"And the name of your front is Transmutual Indemnity, right?" Frank asked. He smiled as Starkey blinked and nervously licked his lips. Frank had caught him off guard at last.

"Maybe you guys deserve your rep after all," Starkey said finally. "Mind telling me how you came to that conclusion?"

"I was willing to believe your story, Mr. Starkey. We visited our uncle Hugh at his office a few times when we were kids, and I don't remember seeing any customers, or signs that there had ever been any," Frank replied. "But I wondered why you were handling this operation. Why not the Network, or Army Intelligence, or even the CIA? There was something in your voice that indicated Hugh's kidnapping was of personal importance to you."

Frank raised his eyebrows. "So I asked myself

why, and only one conclusion makes sense. Assuming your story *is* true, the agency our uncle founded was probably the United States Espionage Resources. Right?"

Starkey nodded sullenly.

"Therefore, his cover is your cover. Transmutual Indemnity," Frank concluded.

"So that's it," said Joe. "You have to get our uncle back because he's one of you. If you wanted our help, all you had to do was ask."

At Joe's remark the smirk returned to Starkey's lips. "That's where you're wrong, pal. Yeah, we want Hunt back, and your help would come in handy. But that's all you're right about because I don't think Hugh Hunt was kidnapped."

"We were there," Frank said, reminding him.

"When I need memory lessons, I'll ask for them," Starkey replied. "Your uncle quit this agency two years ago, no reasons given. Since then a lot of secrets have been ending up with unfriendly governments. It's obvious that someone with inside contacts is behind it all."

"What are you saying?" Joe asked.

Starkey's eyes narrowed, and there was no humor left in his face. "I'm saying your uncle arranged his own kidnapping because it was time to disappear! I'm saying if it hadn't been for you, we'd have caught a master spy—a traitor with the experience to organize his own spy ring, and the knowledge to keep us running in circles while he robs this country blind!"

Starkey jumped up, jabbing his finger in Frank's face.

"And his name is Hugh Hunt!"

Chapter

4

"UNCLE HUGH? A traitor? You're lying!" Joe shouted.

"You and me right now, tough guy," Starkey said, kicking his chair aside as he stood. With both hands, he flagged Joe toward him, ready for a fight.

Tempted, Joe flexed his fists. Then his hands fell open. Even if he could beat Starkey, he knew, it wouldn't get them out of custody. And getting out was the only way they could help their uncle. "Another time," he said. "What do you want us for?"

Starkey brightened. "I like that. Straight to the point." He began to pace the room. "You might be able to help us with a problem. Your 'uncle' wrote the book on this organization. It's his rules we follow, and that puts us at a disadvantage when trying to follow him. He's wise to us and our tricks. We've been trying to put someone close to him to get some hard evidence against him, but—"

"So you don't have any proof that he is a traitor," Frank interrupted.

Starkey scowled. "Kids! Always a smart answer for everything." He tapped a thumb against his stomach. "In my line of work we call it a gut feeling."

I've got the same feeling that we're getting conned here, Frank thought. But he kept that to himself. "Then you want us to get close to our uncle for you," Frank said instead.

"Right," Starkey said. "Right! You *are* good, chum. Ever consider a career in espionage?"

"The way I see it, you've got two more problems," Frank said, ignoring him. "One, we don't know where he is. Kidnappers ran off with him, remember?"

"My people say he's on a flight to San Francisco," Starkey replied calmly. "He has a condominium there. When he checked onto the plane, he wasn't being held against his will. So he's found. What's the second problem?"

"We've only seen our uncle outside of Bayport or New York a few times. What are we supposed to do? Waltz up to him in San Francisco and tell him we decided to drop by for a visit a day after he was kidnapped? Won't that make him a bit suspicious?''

"Risk it," Starkey said. "What you have to remember is that you boys have a rep. Under the circumstances, I don't think Hugh Hunt would expect you to stop looking for him until you found him. He's probably waiting for you to show up. Your problem will be convincing him that you're willing not to pursue his kidnappers. But I have faith in you.''

"Another gut feeling?" Frank quipped. "Can I speak to my brother?''

"Sure," Starkey said.

"Alone?''

"Oh." Starkey nodded and moved to the door. "Sure. Call when you need me." He turned back. "You want the blue light on?''

The cold expression on the Hardys' faces made him grin. "No? Whatever you want." He vanished through the door, and it clicked shut behind him.

For a moment Joe bristled with anger. Then he saw the small, dark mass on the ceiling, hidden in the shadow of the overhead light. It was a microphone. Starkey was off somewhere, planning to listen to every word they were going to say.

"I think Mr. Starkey has made a very convincing case," Frank said. But as he spoke, he pressed his back to the two-way mirror.

Joe leaned next to his brother. He began to

sing, off-key and as loud as he could. As the raucous voice filled the room, Frank whispered in his ear, "It's a setup." Joe nodded and stopped singing.

"I guess you're right," Joe replied. "Starkey's from the government. He wouldn't lie to us, no matter how obnoxious he is." He chuckled to himself as he thought about what Starkey would be thinking right then. "I keep forgetting what the next verse of that song is."

As Frank sang it to him, Joe whispered, "What are we going to do?" But he didn't really need an answer. He knew they had only one choice, to play along with Starkey, go to San Francisco, and do what they could for their uncle.

"We owe it to our country to help bring Uncle Hugh in," Frank answered.

"You're right," Joe said. There was no more need for sign language. He hammered on the door as hard as he could. "Starkey! Get in here!"

Starkey reappeared through the door. "All set? Ready to go?"

"Put us on a plane," Frank replied.

"Not so fast," Starkey said. "I want to get a couple of things straight. You bring your father in on this and I'll tie him in with your uncle and put away both of them. I don't want you talking to the Network, either. This stays between you and me, got it?"

"Clear as a bell," Joe muttered. "When do we go?"

"You'll need a complete briefing, but we can do that on the plane. We have to get you on the first direct flight west."

"How about Air Force One?" Joe asked sweetly. "I hear the President's not using it today."

Starkey frowned. "I'd better go with you," he said. "It would be too bad if you two clowns screwed up."

"You can trust us," Frank said reassuringly. But he was lying.

Though they had visited the city before, San Francisco always seemed slightly alien to Frank and Joe. California was supposed to be warm, the land of sunshine, but San Francisco was always cold and cloudy, with light fog rolling in off the bay.

The city looked strange to them, too. Skyscrapers and antique houses were juxtaposed with no apparent thought to planning. It was like walking into a time warp, and with the unsettling weather, slightly sinister. But there was also an excitement about San Francisco, a sense of magic, and Frank and Joe could easily understand its allure.

They stood on Market Street, studying a map Starkey had given them. He had flown with them to San Francisco and checked them into their hotel, an old stone fortress of a building. He said it had been a favorite of bankers and presidents in

29

the early part of the century. After he had briefed them, he gave them the map and left.

Marked on the map was their uncle's condo. Joe hoped it was in one of the turn-of-the-century houses that dotted the street. He loved those restored homes, which evoked a calmer, simpler era.

"There it is!" Frank said, and Joe's heart sank. The building was modern, made of soulless steel and glass, all sharp edges with none of the gentle frills of the older homes.

Joe couldn't imagine his father's quiet, slightly stuffy friend living in that high-rise, but his name was beside the door next to the word Penthouse.

Frank tugged on the door. "Locked—and no doorman, which is just as well."

Joe studied the lock. It was keyless, with numbers on push buttons. "We can't jimmy this one," he said. "It will open only when you hit the right sequence of numbers."

"You're right," Frank replied. "With nine numbers to choose from, it's mathematically impossible to guess the sequence. We don't even know how many numbers we need."

"Excuse me," said a woman's voice. They turned, and Joe's heart leaped into his throat. She was a beauty, her strawberry-blond hair highlighting her fair skin and bright blue eyes. Joe tried to speak, but the words seemed to catch in his throat. No sound came out.

Joe and Frank stepped aside. The woman

moved past them to the door, and then stood staring at them until they turned their backs and went out on the sidewalk. They stood a few feet away and waited until she worked the lock.

"Did you get a look at *her?*" Joe whispered.

"Quiet!" Frank said. The woman stepped inside, the door closing behind her. Frank sprinted for it. But the door clicked shut before he could reach it.

"Five clicks," Frank said, fingering the lock. "That means she hit five buttons, and each one made a slightly different sound except for the last one, which must have been hit twice in a row. So only four buttons were really used."

"That's why you shut me up!" Joe said. "You were listening!"

"Right," Frank said. He hit all the buttons in order, listening carefully to their sounds. "I think I've got it." Cautiously he pressed the five button. Three. Seven. One, and one again. He turned the door handle.

The door swung open. They stepped cautiously into the building. There were couches in the lobby, but no doorman or any sign of a manager. The elevator had just returned after taking the woman to her floor, and its doors silently glided open. The Hardys stepped inside.

A short ride later the doors opened and they were at their uncle's penthouse.

"Oh, great!" Joe said. He stared at the lock on Hugh's door, a lock identical to the one on the street. "How are we going to get through this one?"

"Maybe we'll get lucky, maybe Uncle Hugh doesn't lock his door," Frank replied. He tried to keep his voice light, but he didn't believe what he said. With a chuckle, Joe played along, turning the door handle.

The door swung open.

"Uncle Hugh?" Joe mumbled in almost a whisper as they stepped inside. No one answered.

"Look at this place," Frank said in awe. The condominium was decorated with simple leather couches. Expensive paintings were hung on two walls. The far walls were blocks of windows, offering vast expanses of San Francisco at a glance. "How can Uncle Hugh afford it?"

"Never mind that!" Joe said, staring out the window. "Take a look at San Francisco from twenty stories up!"

"We're not here to sightsee," Frank reminded him. "Start looking for something—anything—that will clear Uncle Hugh's name." On a coffee table he found a telephone answering machine and switched it on to listen to the messages. The first one was in Russian.

"Or we might find something to hang him with," Joe said grimly. "I don't—"

The sound of something being dragged or pushed across the floor in the next room interrupted him. Silently Joe moved to the door. With a swift kick, he knocked it open, hurling himself into his uncle's bedroom.

It had been ransacked. The clothes from the closet were tossed on the floor—as were the contents of the bureau drawers. A woman stood on the balcony and faced Joe, a sweep of reddish blond hair partially obscuring her eyes.

She was the woman who had come into the building before them.

"Who are you?" Joe asked. "What are you doing here?"

With a smile that made Joe's pulse quicken, the woman pressed back against the balcony railing. Instinctively, Joe knew what she planned. His blood froze.

"No!" he shouted, running for her. "You can't! We're too high up! It's suicide!"

She brushed her hair out of her eyes and turned to face forward. Then she jumped off the balcony into the open arms of death.

Chapter

5

HORRIFIED, JOE RAN to the railing. He didn't want to look at the sidewalk below, didn't want to see the woman lying broken on the concrete. Why did she jump? he wondered. What was her connection to Uncle Hugh? Obviously she had been searching his home, but whose side was she on?

Forcing himself to gaze over the balcony's edge, Joe scanned the sidewalk. There was nothing there. The woman had vanished. Movement at the edge of his vision caught his attention. He turned to see the woman swinging to the roof of the next building on a nylon cord. The cord was tied to the foot of the balcony railing, Joe noticed. She must have had the cord wrapped around her hand as she fell, and used her momentum to swing her to the next roof. All in the seconds since he had entered the room.

He had been tricked, and he didn't like it.

I can still catch her, Joe thought. That building's almost as tall as this one. If I hurry, I'll reach the street at the same time she does, and then we'll find out what this is all about.

"Joe!" Frank said, standing in the bedroom door. "What happened?"

Joe pushed past his brother and bolted for the elevator. "I'll explain later," he said breathlessly. "When I get back." Before Frank could reply, Joe dashed out the front door.

The elevator was back down in the lobby, so Joe frantically ran to the stairs and down to the first floor. He got to the street just in time to see the woman strolling out of the next building. As she glanced around, he ducked back into the doorway. Without noticing him, she walked past him and headed down Market Street, blending into the crowd.

Joe followed her, using the crowd as cover. She glanced over her shoulder often. She seemed to be looking for someone, but her eyes never locked with his in recognition. Twice she looked right at him, but nothing in her face suggested she knew who he was. At last she relaxed and stopped watching her back. Joe began to close the distance between them.

At Grant Avenue the woman turned north, walking for several more blocks. Joe continued to follow, but from the other side of the street, barely aware that the architecture was changing. Slowly he noticed that the shops and doorways were closer together than they had been on the other blocks. The style of clothing was still modern, but the language spoken on the street was no longer English. Nor could Joe read all the signs. Some were still in English, but many others were in Chinese.

He was in Chinatown.

The woman looked at home there, casually ambling down the street as if she didn't have a care in the world. She stopped, looking in the window of a bakery. Was she checking in the window for his reflection? Joe wondered. Quickly he backtracked to a newsstand on the corner of the block, where he bought a paper. All the time he kept his eyes on the woman, who was still staring at the bakery window.

Opening the paper, Joe tore a slit in the back page. Casually, he leaned up against a service doorway and pretended to read. But through the slit he could watch the woman without showing his face. He wished she would move again. The longer he remained in one place, the greater his chances of being discovered.

Two Chinese men sidled out of a tearoom next to the bakery. They were large, taller than the woman, and fat. For a brief second their shapes blotted out hers.

When they passed, she was gone.

Joe crumpled the paper in rage, his abrupt movement causing several people to stop and stare at him. Sighing, he tossed the paper into a trash can and tried to push his way through the crowds. There was no point in secrecy now. The woman's disappearance meant that she had spotted him. She had chosen that single moment, when his view was blocked, to make her move.

There's one consolation, he thought. She can't move in Chinatown any faster than I can because she stands out just as much. She can't have gotten far. I'll catch up to her, and when I do, she had better have some answers.

He glanced into the bakery as he passed it and skidded to a stop. The woman was inside, buying a pastry. She and the clerk were chatting cheerfully. There was no sign that she suspected anything.

Good thing Frank wasn't here to see this, Joe thought. I'd never hear the end of it. He had allowed himself to panic and almost blown his cover. At least it hadn't been a dangerous situation where his panic could have meant the difference between life and death.

The woman came out of the bakery, eating her pastry, and almost bumped into Joe. To his relief, she stared through him as if he weren't there. Letting her get a few steps ahead, he began trailing her again.

She turned off Grant Avenue and started down an alley. Joe waited on the street. If he followed her into the alley, she would spot him for sure. Patiently, he watched until she reached the other end of the alley and turned onto the far street. The instant she turned the corner, he ran into the alley after her.

Two young Chinese in black leather jackets stepped from a doorway along the alley, blocking Joe's way. Before he could back away, two more young men appeared behind him.

They were all younger than Joe, perhaps sixteen years old. But there was a daring viciousness in their faces that startled him. He looked around for a way out, but in the alley all the doors were closed and the windows barred. From one window a face stared out at him. He had seen him before—the clerk in the bakery.

The woman *had* seen him, he realized. Coolly, professionally, she had set this trap for him. And he, fooled into believing he had the situation under control, blundered into it on cue.

"The lady wants you out of the way," said one of the leather-jacketed boys. "She paid us good for it. Too bad for you she didn't say how." There was a click and a flashing arc of silver, and a switchblade appeared, open and ready, in the boy's hand.

Joe threw himself into the boy, grabbing his hand and smashing it down on his knee. The boy's hand flew open, and the knife was thrown across the alley, skittering harmlessly onto the pavement. Joe spun, twisting the boy's arm behind his back. He kicked the kid behind his knee. Off-balance, the boy sprawled onto the ground.

To the other three, Joe said, "Anyone else want to try?"

The boy he had knocked down was still squeezing his wrist and writhing on the ground. The others looked from him to Joe and back to their friend again. They didn't move, until the face in the window shouted something in Chinese.

The youths then charged Joe. He easily knocked their fists aside. But there were three of them. Sooner or later one of their punches would connect. As it was, he felt lucky the kids were street hoods and not martial arts masters. He had met those masters before. Frank, trained in martial arts, could hold his own against them. But Joe and his straightforward fighting style were no match for them.

As he fended off the boys, he glanced around. The way to the other end of the alley was clear. All he needed to do was slow them down long enough to make the run. If he reached the street, he'd be safe.

Suddenly Joe lashed out, catching the nearest boy with a jab to his jaw. The boy fell back, and Joe swung his arm, catching a second kid on the ear. The third took a clip in the chest from Joe's elbow, and the boy howled in pain.

Joe spun and ran. But on his second step, someone clasped him around his ankle, pitching him over. He twisted as he fell, and the face of the fourth boy, the one he had taken the knife from, smiled at him. The boy's hand was clamped on Joe's leg. Then Joe's temple smacked the pavement, and darkness began to fold over him.

A great weight crushed him into the ground, pulling him back to consciousness. The other boys, Joe realized. He opened his eyes, and wished he hadn't. The first boy had found his switchblade. Darkness swirled before Joe's eyes.

But before the darkness totally swallowed Joe up, he saw the knife plunging down.

Chapter

6

FRANK HARDY EYED his watch. An hour had passed since his brother left the condominium. At first Frank hadn't been worried. It was like Joe to act on impulse and give no explanation. And even in a strange city, Joe was more than capable of taking care of himself.

Frank had continued to search his uncle's apartment. Aside from the phone messages, he found nothing unusual. But now as the minutes continued to tick past, Frank became increasingly concerned about his brother's safety.

He waited another fifteen minutes, reading an article in a magazine that he had found on his uncle's coffee table. Still no sign of Joe. He set the magazine on the table and arranged it the way he had found it.

What was keeping him? Frank wondered. If

43

only Joe had said where he was going! He decided to give his brother five more minutes, and he walked onto the balcony to see if he could spot him returning.

It was late in the afternoon now, and there were heavy crowds of people below. More than a day, he thought, since his uncle had been kidnapped. As sharp-eyed as he was, Frank couldn't pick a single face out of that throng, not from that height.

Even the cars were too small to be identified. He stretched out his hand, playing at picking up a black limousine that seemed to him to be the size of a toy. His hand closed on empty air, and he chuckled.

The chuckle stuck in his throat as the limousine pulled up to the curb in front of the building he was in. Two men in dark suits climbed out, followed by a white-haired man. Frank couldn't see his face, but he knew the white-haired man by the way he moved.

It was his uncle Hugh! He was coming up.

Frank ran through the bedroom and living room and slipped out of the apartment. An arrow glowed over the elevator door, signaling that the elevator was on its way up. He ran back into the penthouse. Where could he hide? He thought of closets and immediately dismissed the idea. If suspicious, his uncle and his companions were certain to look in them. Outside, the elevator arrived with the gentle ring of a bell, but a hiding place still eluded Frank. How could he explain his presence to his uncle? He couldn't, he realized. If he tried, his uncle's suspicions would be aroused. Then there would be nothing Frank or Joe could do to help him.

As the outer lock clicked, Frank decided to hide under the bed. It was obvious and uncomfortable, but they wouldn't immediately see him there. Reaching the bedroom, he dropped to his hands and knees and rolled.

He slammed into a plank of solid wood beneath the bedspread.

It was a platform bed, and there was no room for him to hide under it. The clicking of the front door lock stopped, and the door swung open.

Frank lay on the bedroom floor as a Russian entered the apartment, with his uncle Hugh and another Russian behind him. The first man seemed agitated, flexing his hands before him and rolling his eyes to the ceiling. If Frank moved, or if the Russian lowered his eyes, he would be discovered. Frank held his breath.

"Speak English," Frank's uncle ordered. But both Russians continued jabbering angrily in their native tongue. Finally the break Frank needed came. As they argued, the Russians turned their backs on the bedroom door. In that instant, Frank was on his feet.

He slipped inside the bedroom closet and silently slid the door to within an inch of being closed. Now he could hear what was being said in the other room.

"I told you to speak English, Feodor," Hugh Hunt said. He sounded angry now, too. The voices grew softer, and Frank could hear water being run as glasses were clinked together. They were in the kitchen. For a moment Frank considered making a dash for the front door. If they were all in the kitchen, he could make it. Maybe.

Too iffy. Frank decided to stay where he was.

Back in the living room Feodor said, "*Da,* we will speak English for you now, Peregrine." There was a hint of mockery in his thick Russian voice.

"Don't call me that," Hunt said. His voice sounded closer now; probably he was in the living room as well. "I haven't gone by that name in years. Not since I retired from the business."

"But you are *not* retired, are you?" asked a second Russian voice. This one, like the first, sounded strange to Frank, as if the owners were putting on the accents. "You are back in business, *da?* And thanks to our poison, you are working for us."

Frank gasped. His uncle wasn't a traitor after all, he realized. He was being *forced* to work for the Russians, under threat of death.

Except, he thought, Starkey suspected him before he was poisoned. Other things puzzled

Frank. Why did the Russians call his uncle Peregrine? The mystery grew deeper and deeper.

"Silence, Oleg!" Feodor barked.

"I'm not sure I should pull this job for you," Hunt said. The anger had drained from his voice, to be replaced by the cool confidence Frank knew so well. "What assurance do I have that the antidote to your poison really exists?"

Feodor laughed. "You do not. But you must trust us, no? If another forty-eight hours pass, and you do not receive the antidote . . ."

"All right," Hunt replied. "I'll do your dirty work for you. But if you're lying about the antidote, I swear I won't die alone." There was no threat in his voice. Frank could tell that as far as his uncle was concerned, he had merely stated a fact.

"We do not lie," Feodor said with a hint of fear. "Come. Let us make our plans."

"Right," his uncle said, and Frank was startled to hear him moving closer. "The sooner we get this over with, the better."

"You have a plan already?"

"If your diagram of the museum is accurate, yes," Hunt replied. "Here, I'll give you the rundown, so you can learn your parts."

Three sets of footsteps grew louder. With a start, Frank realized they were entering the bedroom. As quietly as he could, Frank shifted in the closet so that he could peer through the crack.

They hadn't heard him. His uncle stood in front of the bed next to a tall, dark-haired man with an eye patch and a shorter man. Frank recognized them from the description Joe had given him. They were the men who had kidnapped their uncle.

Hunt eyed the room and frowned as if he had noticed something was out of place. But the Russians paid no attention. "We are not to be directly involved," the man with the eye patch said. Feodor, by his voice, Frank judged. "We told you that."

"The museum has too much security," Hunt said. "I can't get it all, so you'll have to take out some of it. The rest I can handle by myself." He smirked. "Of course, I could always bring in some outside help if you like."

The idea clearly distressed the Russians, and Frank stifled a laugh at the sight of the color draining from their faces.

"What is the plan?" Feodor asked with an air of resignation.

As his uncle walked to the closet and slid the door open, Frank backed into the shadows. A trace of light flickered over Frank's face while his uncle reached into the pocket of a suit and pulled out a folded sheet of paper. Then the door slid halfway closed again.

Had his uncle seen him?

Feodor paced impatiently as Hunt unfolded the paper. The dark-haired Russian stood at the balcony door, then turned to face the room. Frank squatted in the closet, trying to stay out of sight. It was useless. All Feodor had to do was look in his direction. There was nowhere for Frank to run or hide.

To Frank's relief, Feodor turned again to look out the balcony. He stared down at the street and, with a grunt of anger, stiffened.

Tied to the railing was a long nylon cord!

Feodor spun around, drawing his pistol with the silencer. "Someone has been here," he said darkly. "Search the apartment." Then his eyes narrowed. He peered into the darkness of the closet.

"Come out," he ordered, waving the pistol. "Hands up."

Frank stepped from the closet with his hands cupped behind his head. If his uncle recognized him, it didn't show in the man's face.

Feodor's eyes narrowed. "Come here." Frank stepped slowly toward him.

"Look out!" the Russian named Oleg screamed. Feodor jerked his gaze to Oleg, and in that instant, Frank's hands came out from behind his head.

The wire hanger Frank had concealed behind him flew like a boomerang from his hand to Feodor's face. Frank knew the slap of metal couldn't hurt the Russian, but Feodor stepped back, stunned, as the hanger struck his forehead.

With a savage cry, Frank leaped forward, kicking the pistol from Feodor's hands. He spun quickly, smashing his other foot into the big Russian's shoulder. Feodor toppled. Frank dived at the fallen pistol and scooped it up.

The click of a gun hammer being drawn sounded behind him. "Please set the pistol down," Oleg said.

Sighing, Frank turned the gun over to Feodor, who knelt before him with one hand out. There was murder in Feodor's eyes.

Without a word, Feodor pressed the pistol against Frank's chest.

"No!" Hunt shouted. Feodor glared at him, and Oleg swung his pistol to cover him. "Don't worry. I won't give you any trouble," he continued calmly. "I just don't want you to kill him here. Take him somewhere else."

Feodor nodded and smiled. Oleg strolled to the balcony and pulled the cord free from the railing. In moments he had Frank bound with it. Frank's uncle watched impassively, but made no move to intervene.

"We will drop him off a bridge," Feodor suggested. "Just one more soul taking his own life."

The three men laughed and led Frank from the apartment.

Chapter

7

WHEN JOE HARDY woke, the air smelled of fresh-brewed coffee, and his head was throbbing. He could feel the rough rope that was wrapped around his wrists, which were tied behind him. But he couldn't feel his hands. They were numb because the circulation had been cut off by the rope. His feet were pressed together, and he couldn't move them apart. So they had to be bound, too.

He felt lucky to be alive.

He was indoors, lying on an old Persian carpet, staring at a hundred-year-old black marble fireplace. Must be one of the fine old houses of San Francisco, he thought. Everything he could see had the look of a finely crafted antique. Everything except the woman.

She lounged in an armchair, legs crossed, sipping a cup of coffee. She had changed into stretch pants and a loose yellow sweatshirt that brought out the blond in her hair. Her bright blue eyes were fixed on Joe, and the corners of her mouth were curled up slightly.

"Joe Hardy," she said. "You're finally awake."

"How—?" he began, until he saw her dangling his wallet. "So you know my name. Do I get to know yours?"

She giggled, charmingly pressing her fingers to her lips to smother the sound. In a voice that reminded Joe of crystal wind chimes, she said, "Call me Charity. We're going to be very good friends."

"No, thanks. I've met your friends," Joe said. "I'm not sure I could take another party with them. By the way, where are they?"

"Oh," she drawled with a tone of disinterest. "They're around here somewhere. You really did make a bad impression on them, you know. It was all I could do to keep them from using you as a punching bag."

"Sorry I wasn't more cooperative. When did you spot me?"

"As soon as we left Hugh Hunt's," said Charity. "I was watching for you. But you're very good. A couple of times I thought I had lost you, but you were always there. You forced me to resort to the hired help."

"Sorry."

"Don't be. Now that we've met, Joe, perhaps we can work together."

"On what?" he asked.

She gently patted his cheek. "You don't have to pretend with me, Joe. Aren't we both after the same thing?"

"Yes, I guess we are," Joe said. "Whose side are you on?"

"On *my* side, darling. Of course." At the sound of a loud buzzer, her smile faded. "I'm afraid I have some other business to take care of, Joe. When I come back, you can fill me in on Hugh Hunt's plans. You won't go away, will you?"

Joe rolled onto his back and smiled bitterly at her. Blowing him a kiss, she left the room, locking the door behind her, and walked down the stairs.

Uncle Hugh's plans? he wondered. What had the woman meant? He sensed that she held the key to this game of spies, and he had until she returned to find that key.

Joe curled up, bringing his knees to his chest, and strained to slip his hands under him. They were bound too tightly to slip easily over his hips. He wriggled, but it was no use. Joe was stronger than his brother, but Frank was the more agile of the two. Joe wished he had that agility now.

He tried to remember how Frank would do it. Relaxation and concentration, that was the key.

He calmed himself, took a deep breath, and held it. Then he let all the air out, tensed his hips and relaxed his arms as much as he could, and jerked his hands forward.

Joe's hands slipped past his hips and slid to his ankles. Digging his fingers behind his heels, he forced off his shoes. His hands easily rounded his heels and toes. At last, his hands were in front of him, where he could use them.

He fumbled at the knots in the ropes binding his ankles and clenched his teeth in silent frustration. His fingers were too numb to feel the knots. If he wanted to escape, he had to free his hands first and get the blood back into them.

Wrapping his arms around his knees and pressing them to his chest, Joe rolled back and forth on his spine, faster and faster, until he lurched forward onto the balls of his feet. Hands in front of him, he toppled forward. His hands struck the floor and broke his fall, and he steadied himself. Now balanced on hands and feet, Joe straightened his legs. Slowly he raised his head and spine until he was standing up.

He heard footsteps and voices on the stairs. Charity was coming back up, and she wasn't alone. He had no time to free himself.

He clumsily hopped across the floor, and his weight smashing up and down made the old wooden floor quiver when he left the Persian rug. The voices and footsteps halted at the crashing, and someone on the stairs shouted his name. Then the footsteps thundered up the stairs—they were running now. Joe knew his only chance was to get to the door before they did.

His eyes fixed on the doorknob and the lock an inch below it. He hopped closer and closer, his hands stretched out.

The knob turned and the door began to open.

With one last, desperate lunge, Joe rammed himself into the door, slamming it shut. Before whoever was on the other side of the door could react, Joe turned the lock.

Fists pounded angrily on the door. "Joe!" Charity called. "Open up! We're not going to hurt you!"

Joe ignored her, scanning the room. He spied a lamp made from a glass tube, an imitation of the old glass-topped candleholders used before electric lights became common. It was beautiful, he thought, but beauty was of no use to him now. He smashed the lamp to the floor, watching the glass shatter into fragments.

"Joe!" Charity cried again, and the pounding at the door grew louder. "Go downstairs and get the key," she said softly to someone on the stairs.

Good, Joe thought. That would buy him time. He crouched and straightened the base of the lamp. A jagged splinter of glass jutted up from it. Quickly he ran the rope around his wrists up and down the edge of the glass. He winced when it brushed his skin, but he ignored the pain. The rope was fraying, loosening.

All at once, it fell away. His hands were free.

He opened and closed his fists, stretching his fingers until a bit of feeling returned. The footsteps were coming back up the stairs, and his time was running out. He grabbed a piece of glass and sawed the rope away from his ankles, then he stood and slipped his loafers on, his fists ready. His movements would be restricted in the tight space of the room, but Joe was ready to go down fighting.

"I can't find it," came a raspy voice from the hall. It was the voice of the boy who had pulled the knife on him in the alley.

"You're useless, Tony," Charity replied. "*I'll* get it."

Joe glanced around the room, ready to put the extra time to good use. But there were burglar bars on all the windows, and only two doors, one leading to a bedroom and the other leading to the hall. There was no way out.

He looked into the bedroom. An old four-poster bed stood there, and a chest of drawers. But there was little else in the room. The windows were also barred. He looked outside.

The room was four stories up, too far for him to jump even if he could remove the bars. It was one of the houses built for rich San Franciscans in the last century, he realized. Nothing but a den of thieves now, Joe thought.

"Enough!" a harsh voice cried from the stairs. The voice had a thick Chinese accent, and sounded older than Tony.

The crack of splintering wood caught Joe's attention, and he glanced back into the other room. The wood paneling of the door was being broken into small pieces by the heel of someone's hand.

There was one final crack, and the hand moved through the hole in the door, groping for the lock.

Chapter

8

THE DOOR CRASHED OPEN.

It was the man who had been in the alley window, and he stepped cautiously into the room. Pieces of the broken lamp and strips of rope littered the floor, but there was no sign of Joe. Charity and Tony appeared in the doorway behind him.

Seeing the damage to the door, Charity's eyes narrowed angrily. "What do you think you're doing, Kwan?"

"Shhh!" the older Chinese man said. He waved a thumb at the bedroom. "He's in there." Stepping sideways, he stepped through the bedroom doorway. His mouth dropped open.

"The Hardy boy is gone," Kwan said sullenly.

"It's not possible," Charity answered. "This

section of the house is sealed up tight." She pushed past Kwan and slumped over when she saw a large square of wallpaper cut from the bedroom wall. Joe's glass shard lay abandoned next to the square.

"What is that?" Kwan demanded, pointing at the hole in the wall.

"An old air shaft," she said. "It used to be for ventilation. It was papered over when the building changed to air conditioning."

"Where does it go?"

Charity frowned. "The roof end of the shaft is plugged up. The other end comes out in the basement."

"He's downstairs!" Tony shouted. "Come on!"

Back aching, Joe Hardy dropped from the shaft to the basement floor. So far, so good, he thought. The shaft had been a tight fit, but, bracing his feet against one wall of the shaft and his back against the opposite wall, he had managed to work his way to the bottom. There was no stampede from above, which he hoped meant they hadn't discovered his escape. He switched on a light and scanned the basement. Shadowy and damp, it contained only a clothes washer and dryer. The rest of the basement was unused, a place to store empty boxes, with no windows.

He dashed up the stairs to the ground floor,

spun on his heel, and ran to the front door. It wasn't locked.

The pounding of footsteps greeted him as he stepped back into the entryway. They were coming after him, but it didn't matter. The front door was only a few feet away, and they would never be able to get down three flights of stairs before he made it to the street.

Except, he realized, he hadn't found what he needed to find. What was the woman's connection with his uncle Hugh? He couldn't leave before he found out.

The footsteps sounded louder. They were probably on the third landing. He dashed to the room off the hallway and peeked in. It was a study—Charity's study, he deduced from the purse on the desk. The desk appeared to be as old as all the other furniture in the house, a monstrous carved-oak banker's desk. The footsteps reached the second landing. He had only a moment to decide what to do.

He ran to the front door again and flung it open, then doubled back down the hall. As Tony leaped over the last banister and landed on the rug at the foot of the stairs, Joe ducked into the study and crossed his fingers.

Tony shouted something in Chinese, then said, "He got away." He pointed an accusing finger at Charity. "This is your fault."

Charity glanced at him angrily, and turning to

Kwan, she said, "Remind your boy who's employing whom here. And do it on your way out."

"What about this Joe Hardy?" Tony demanded.

"Get out there and find him!" Charity said explosively. "Must I do all your thinking for you? He can't have gotten far. Find him and bring him back. Go!"

Kwan nodded and Tony left, slamming the door behind him. "Your activities have been compromised?"

"I don't think so," Charity replied. "He didn't have time. But let me check."

Joe slipped across the study and behind the desk as Charity backed into the same room. Her attention was focused on Kwan, so she hadn't seen him. He crawled beneath the desk and pressed against the back of it.

Charity walked behind the desk as he pulled his hands out of sight. The center drawer opened, casting its shadow over him. "No," Charity said. "Everything's still here, in order. He didn't touch it."

"Then you will continue?" asked Kwan.

"Of course," she replied with a soft laugh. "One more obstacle isn't going to faze me."

"Of course," Kwan said. Joe heard his steps trail away, and then the front door opened and closed. Kwan had left.

"Of course," Charity repeated after a long

pause. Then the drawer slid shut. Joe could see her face as she stepped away from the desk, but she didn't look down. Without another word, she left the study and went back up the stairs.

After a few minutes Joe slid out from under the desk. There was no sound anywhere in the house. He tried the drawer and found it locked. On top of the desk was a pencil holder, and in it a few pens and a letter opener. Joe took the opener and rammed it into the space between the drawer and the desk.

He pushed down, using the opener as a lever. The drawer bolt popped out of the desk, and Joe pulled the drawer open.

Inside the drawer were a dozen photographs of a glass museum case. Inside the glass case was a golden crown.

He took a magnifying glass from the drawer and studied the photos carefully. Below the glass was a small plaque. "Incan Crown," it read. "C. 1350." It went on with a brief explanation of the history of the Inca nation that had conquered much of South America before the arrival of the Spaniards. Then it described the Inca craft of gold working that had resulted in the fine crown made from a single thread of gold braided back and forth on itself. The crown was then decorated with polished stones. Joe could see nothing else on the photographs.

He turned them over. On the back of one was a

sloppily scrawled note: "Carlyle Museum. Est. val. $100,000." He slipped the photos back into the drawer and closed it, more puzzled now than when he had begun. It was obvious to him that the woman intended to steal the crown, but what did that have to do with his uncle Hugh? Watching for any signs of Charity, Joe crept from the study, down the hall, and out the front door. Kwan and Tony were nowhere to be seen. Quickly Joe checked his map and began to run in the direction of Market Street.

From a second-story window Charity watched and smiled.

As inconspicuously as he could, Frank Hardy struggled with the cord that bound his wrists in front of him. Standing in the lobby with Frank, the Russians paid little attention to him. Instead, they watched the early-evening street, waiting until it was relatively clear of people so they could smuggle him out of his uncle Hugh's building. "You stay here," Feodor said to Hunt. "Better you not be seen with us. Who knows who is watching? We pick you up night after tomorrow night."

"You want me cooped up for two whole days?" he replied with some amazement. He spoke directly to Feodor, avoiding Frank's gaze. Oleg stepped behind Frank, nuzzling the boy's ribs with his gun, and Frank stopped straining on the cord. "Just what do you expect me to do all that time?"

"Stay. Study plan," said Feodor. "You have one chance to make it work. If you fail—"

"I don't get the antidote, and I die," Hugh continued. "Don't worry. I plan to live."

Feodor grinned. "Is good. We study plan, too. Oleg, you have plan?"

Proudly Oleg patted his coat breast pocket with his free hand. He put his face close to Frank's, and Frank could feel the Russian's moist breath on his ear. "We have plan for you, too," Oleg whispered and dug the gun deeper into Frank's ribs. "You make noise, we finish you right here. Bang, bang."

With a curt nod, Hugh Hunt vanished back into the building. Frank couldn't believe his eyes. He understood why his uncle would pretend not to recognize him, but the man was showing no interest in rescuing him. His uncle was not going to help him.

Oleg jostled Frank over to the limousine at the curb. Feodor walked ahead, carefully checking the block for witnesses. There were none. He opened the back door of the limousine, shoved Frank inside, and slid in beside him. As Frank righted himself in the seat, Oleg moved around to the driver's seat.

"Why all this fooling around?" Frank asked. "Why not just kill me and get it over with?"

"Kill you?" Feodor said and chuckled. "We not kill you. You have . . ." He paused, thinking. "Sports accident! You swim, eh?"

"Sure," Frank said.

Feodor laughed again. "Maybe you live, then. We give you little bump on head, let you jump. Ever go off Golden Gate Bridge? No, eh? Water very cold, wake you up maybe. Current very strong, drag you out to sea." He shrugged. "Maybe not. You swim well, maybe you make it."

The Russian's mirthful belly laugh made Frank's skin crawl as the nylon rope bit into his wrists. He looked around for a way to escape and found nothing.

Nothing except the figure charging down the street behind them.

Breathless from running, Joe Hardy neared his uncle Hugh's apartment. He hoped Frank was still there. Questions kept bouncing around in his head. But between his brother and himself, he felt sure they could sort out the answers.

He stopped suddenly and gaped at the limousine passing him. In the front was the short man who had driven the getaway car in New York. There in the back, as he expected, was the man with the eye patch.

With Frank.

"Frank!" he shouted as he turned and ran after the limo. It was no use. On the now-quiet street, the limo easily pulled away from him. Gasping for breath, he came to a halt and watched the limo vanish into the distance.

A car sped up to him, and he waved his arms to flag it over. But the car continued by without slowing down. Another car passed, and then a motorcycle. The cyclist, his face hidden behind a black visor, turned his head to watch Joe wave, but both car and cyclist continued on.

Joe began to run again, but he knew it was hopeless. Without transportation, he had no way of catching up to the limo.

Then he smiled. The cyclist had pulled into a parking space just ahead; he got off the bike and was walking into a pharmacy, leaving the keys in the ignition.

In seconds Joe was on the big machine, turning the key. As it roared to life, he flipped off the brake and ripped onto the street. The owner ran out of the pharmacy and stared silently as Joe followed the limo. If it had not been an emergency, Joe would never have stolen anything. But he also knew his brother's life hung in the balance, and to save his brother he would take any risk.

He spotted the limo as it was pulling onto Geary Street. He followed as it became an expressway and then switched back to a street. In vain, Joe searched for an opening.

There were too many people and cars around. If the Russians started shooting at him, too many people could get hurt. He could see Frank moving in the backseat of the limo. For the moment, at least, his brother was all right.

At Park Presidio Boulevard, the limo switched on its headlights and turned north. Joe was still behind it. They followed the boulevard to Doyle Drive, heading northwest. In the distance Joe could see the lit-up Golden Gate Bridge, which led from San Francisco to Marin County in the north. No matter that he had seen the famous bridge before; he was overcome by its beauty once again.

And right then he understood why the Russians were going there. He hoped he was wrong, but instinctively knew he was right. And he knew that if Frank were to be rescued, he had to do it right then.

As they pulled onto the bridge, Joe shifted into high gear and sped past the limousine. Neither the short man nor the one-eyed man noticed. They were watching for the perfect spot to pull over and shove Frank into the merciless water below. Frank probably didn't spot me, either, Joe thought. I just hope he'll be quick on his feet.

When he was one hundred feet ahead of the car, Joe slammed his heel to the pavement and jerked the front end of the cycle off the ground. The bike spun, the front wheel slammed down again, and then he was racing head-on toward the limousine.

For what seemed like an eternity, the cyle sped toward the limo, Joe's eyes fixed slightly above the headlights so the glare wouldn't blind him. Joe swerved the bike to the right of the car seconds before it would have collided with it. Tires locked and screeched, and the cycle flew into a skid, throwing Joe at the car, just as he had planned. The driver's window was open, and Joe reached through it, locking his arm around the short man's neck.

The car swerved and weaved as Oleg gasped for breath. In the back Frank slammed his elbow into Feodor's chin, stunning him.

The limo crashed into the side of the bridge, knocking Joe to the pavement. With a groan, he picked himself up. The front end of the limo was twisted against a steel railing, and no one inside was moving. Then Frank moaned, and Oleg and Feodor stirred.

"Come on, Frank," Joe called. "Let's get out of here."

"Just a minute," Frank said. He leaned over the front seat and reached into Oleg's coat. His hand came out holding a folded sheet of paper.

"Got it!" he said as he climbed out of the car. "Let's go."

As they ran across the bridge, a bullet *spanged* off a girder. Frank looked over his shoulder. Feodor and Oleg were out of the car, shooting at them. "They've almost got our range, Joe," he said. "We'll never make it."

Joe eyed the dark waters below. "There's one chance," he said.

"Too dangerous," Frank said. "Do you know how many people die every year by jumping off the Golden Gate Bridge? If we get caught in the undertow—" He cut himself off as he glanced over his shoulder. Feodor was down on one knee, taking careful aim.

"Right," said Joe. He knew that look in his brother's eye, the look that said one chance in a million was better than no chance at all. "Let's do it."

As another shot whizzed by, the Hardys lunged over the railing and plummeted with twin splashes into the deadly bay.

Frank Hardy swam to the surface, spat out water, and gulped in air. Treading water, he strained to pull the cord from his wrists. Above, he saw the Russians, straining their eyes to pick the Hardys out against the inky darkness of the bay. It was too dark, he knew, and the flashing red lights approaching from the distance would quickly drive the Russians off. "Stay low, Joe," he whispered. "The cops are on their way."

There was no reply. "Joe?" he said louder. Still the only sound was the fierce lapping of waves. Frank peered across the night sea. Nothing else bobbed there.

Joe had not come up for air after the dive. He was gone.

Chapter
9

JUST UNDER THE surface of the water, something moved. A head bobbed up, then sank again. Joe!

Frank called his brother's name, but there was no answer. He hoped Joe was only unconscious, knocked out by the impact. But Frank had to wake him quickly, before he drowned or was swept out to sea. Water flowed around them, pulling them gently toward the mouth of San Francisco Bay. The farther they moved, the faster they went, dragged relentlessly in the murderous undertow. A few more minutes, Frank knew, and they would both be beyond help.

Taking in a lungful of air, Frank dived underwater. The cord hindered his movements, making it difficult to swim. He wished for more light, but none came. In that undersea night he could see nothing but shades of gray and black.

71

A dozen feet away a dark, man-shaped patch rose. Joe again, Frank guessed, rising for perhaps the last time. Frank kicked his feet and propelled himself against the current. His lungs burned and air forced itself up into his throat, but he kept his mouth closed. The dark patch, helpless against the current, pulled away from him. Frank kicked frantically, building up speed. His vision blurred and his lungs ached from the effort of holding in the air. If he should open his mouth, he knew, the sea would rush in, and he would never make it to the surface again.

He slammed into Joe, but Joe didn't move. Frank dived again, coming up with his shoulder under the small of Joe's back, pushing his brother upward.

They broke the surface, and Frank gasped desperately for air. But Joe was rolling away, already beginning to sink again. Without his hands free, there was no way for Frank to keep Joe afloat. Frank grabbed his brother by the belt. Kicking to keep himself above water, he jerked Joe toward him as hard as he could and then let him go.

With as much strength and leverage as he could muster in the water, Frank punched Joe in the stomach.

Reflexively, Joe gasped, a geyser of water and air rushing from his lungs. Shaken to semiconsciousness, he hacked the rest of the fluid out with a fierce cough and thrashed in the water.

"Joe!" Frank cried. "Wake up! Please wake up!"

At last Joe opened his eyes and stopped slapping the water. Like Frank, he started to kick his feet to keep himself afloat. "Frank! Where are we? What—" He looked at the bridge and suddenly remembered. "The Russians!"

Red lights spun and flashed on the bridge. The police were there. A spotlight went on, shining down and skimming along the water.

"It's a sure bet the Russians are gone by now," Frank said. "And we had better be out of here, too. It won't do us or Uncle Hugh any good, having to explain this to the police."

"Right," Joe agreed. They bobbed beneath the water as the searchlight neared. It touched the place where they had been and moved on. They surfaced again. "It's only a couple hundred feet to shore and the current should be moving in that direction. Let's go."

"Joe? Would you mind?" Frank held out his arms. With a chuckle, Joe untied his brother. "Thanks."

As the searchlight began another circuit, they swam and came ashore in the shadow of Fort Point. The old fort was closed, and there was no one else around. Exhausted, they crawled onto the beach and collapsed there. The searchlight still beamed off the bridge. No one suspected they had survived.

"This could be a break," Frank said. "The Russians are probably watching the cops. I hope they'll think we're finished when we're not found. That would make it easier for us to wreck their plan."

"What is their plan, anyway?" Joe asked. Soaked to the skin, he shivered in the chill night air. "I know they're planning to steal an old Inca crown, but aside from that—"

"What?" Frank interrupted, dumbfounded. "Where did you learn that?"

Joe smiled. It wasn't often that he was able to surprise Frank. "There's a woman involved in this, the one we saw at the elevator. Her name's Charity. I followed her and got to see some photos she has of the crown. She wanted to know what Uncle Hugh's plans for stealing it were."

"Then she's not on Uncle Hugh's side," Frank said. "So whose side is she on? Starkey's? If that's the case, why didn't he tell us?"

"Don't expect him to tell us anything," Joe said. "Unless it's a lie. Something's not on the level about him."

"Something's off about all of this," Frank said. "Like those Russians. Sometimes they speak broken English, and sometimes they speak as well as you or I. It's like they're playacting."

Frank's face grew more serious. "I wish I could figure out how Uncle Hugh fits into all this. I learned the Russians fed him a slow-acting poison, and if he does this job for them, they'll give him the antidote. So it seems he's been forced into helping them. But he didn't lift a finger to help me when the Russians carted me off. If you hadn't shown up—"

"You would have thought of something," Joe said. "I guess the key to this whole thing is the crown, but I can't believe the Russians are only interested in this old treasure. If only we knew where it was, we could get a good look at it and then—"

It was Frank's turn to smile. "Funny you should mention it." He pulled a crumpled, soggy piece of paper from his back pocket and spread it out as best he could on the grass.

"That's what you dragged out of the little Russian's coat before you got out of the limo," Joe said. "What is it?" he asked, taking out a small penlight.

"A photocopy of the floor plans for the Carlyle Museum of History, complete with instructions on how to bypass all the security. Uncle Hugh figured it out."

"Look at this place," Joe said and shone the light across the paper. "Lasers, heat sensors, air pressure sensors. It's more like a fortress than a museum. Ever notice how this case gets screwier the deeper into it we get?"

"Boy, have I," Frank began and then froze. Near the wall of the fort, something snapped.

"Someone's there," Frank whispered. "We have to get out of here." He snatched up the paper and stuffed it into his pocket again. Another snap.

Frank and Joe crawled across the grass, hugging the ground. At the wall they heard a match scratch, and a man touched the flame to the tip of a cigarette. Shadows cast by the flame blacked out his eyes and made him unrecognizable. He tossed the match down and ground it out with his heel.

The glow of the cigarette slowly pulsing over his face, he walked straight at the Hardys. From a shoulder holster hidden beneath his coat, he drew a gun.

"Hit him!" Frank whispered. As if a single mind directed them, Frank and Joe, hidden by the night, lunged at the armed man.

Headlights flared on, catching them in midlunge, and the man held his revolver aimed at the Hardys. He stepped toward the boys, signaling them to raise their hands.

Frank backed into Joe's shadow and crushed the paper completely into his pocket before he lifted his hands. No one noticed.

The man with the gun jostled Frank and Joe, roughly pushing them toward the waiting car. "You've had enough fun for one day," he said. "Starkey wants to talk to you."

"Care for some tea?" Starkey said. "It'll help drive the chill out."

"Sure," Frank replied. His clothes had mostly

dried on the ride from Fort Point to the Van Ness Avenue hotel district, but he was still cold. Joe and Frank each sat on a bed in their hotel room; Starkey leaned against the wall. In the corner the man with the revolver watched a movie on cable television and paid no attention to them.

Another man poured two cups of tea from a large silver pot and handed them to Frank and Joe. "So," Starkey said. "What did you find out?"

"You answer a question first, okay?" said Frank. "Who's Peregrine?"

"Well, well," Starkey said, amused. "Since you ask, that was Hugh Hunt's code name when he worked in Eastern Europe. Why? Someone mention it?"

"The Russians," Frank began.

"So Hunt *is* working for them," Starkey said excitedly. "He probably started working for them when he was Peregrine."

"I don't think so," Frank said. "They were taunting him with the name. They're extorting his help."

"To do what?" Starkey asked.

"Something to do with a crown at the Carlyle Museum," Joe said. "They're planning to snatch it."

"Let me get this straight," Starkey said excitedly. "Hugh Hunt and the Russians are planning to rob a museum?"

"It looks that way," Frank admitted. "But

don't you understand? They're forcing him into it!"

"But Hugh Hunt *is* working with the Russians, and they *are* planning to knock over the Carlyle Museum, right?" Starkey insisted.

With a resigned sigh, Frank replied, "Yes."

Starkey opened his jacket and pulled a small tape recorder from an inside pocket. "That's all we need," he said. "Independent verification that Hugh Hunt is working with an enemy government."

"You haven't listened to a thing we said," shouted Joe.

"Sure I have, tough guy," Starkey said, smirking. "Mickey!" The man with the gun shut off the television, turned, and drew his revolver.

"These boys have outlived their usefulness," Starkey said. With a smile, the man called Mickey took aim at Frank and Joe and cocked the hammer on his gun.

Chapter
10

"YOU'RE KIDDING," FRANK said, but the cruel glint in Starkey's eyes told Frank that he meant it.

"This is a secret organization," Starkey replied. "We can't have a couple of kids running around with all our secrets, can we?" He glared at Joe. "Keep those hammy fists where we can see them, kid, and don't do anything stupid. Mickey here knows every way there is to kill a man. He'll be very quick and painless, and he won't leave a mark."

"How very convenient for you," Joe muttered.

"Or he can make it very messy if you get on his bad side," Starkey continued. "On second thought, do something stupid. I'd like to see that."

"Anyone ever tell you how thoroughly unpleasant you are?" Frank said.

Starkey grinned. "It's the job."

"There's no way out of this, is there?"

"No, I'm afraid there isn't. If you somehow managed to get out of this room, which I doubt you could do, I have my agents all over the hotel. You'd never make it to the front door."

"I almost wouldn't mind going if I knew why you're doing this, Starkey."

"Well, I'm not going to tell you. Anything else I can do?"

"Another cup of tea?" Frank asked.

"You think you get a last request, just like in the movies?" Starkey shrugged. "All right, go ahead. Just one cup, though."

"Thanks," Frank said. Picking up his cup, he moved toward Mickey. The gunman drew his revolver as Frank approached, keeping him covered. Frank swung in a wide arc around Mickey, staying out of the gunman's reach. At the table Frank picked up the teapot.

"More tea, Joe?" Frank asked.

"I hate tea," Joe said sullenly. His rage-filled eyes fixed on Starkey, who was ignoring him.

Furtively, Frank studied Mickey. The man looked like a professional quarterback. And Frank guessed that Mickey could withstand any attack Frank could make.

"Sure, you want some tea," Frank said.

"I don't *like* tea," Joe said. It was true. He hadn't touched the cup Starkey gave him.

"Sure you do," Frank insisted, watching as Mickey snuffed out a cigarette in an ashtray on top of the television. "Pass me your cup, Joe."

"Frank, I don't want any tea," Joe maintained.

"If the kid doesn't want any tea, he doesn't want any tea," Starkey barked. "Get on with it."

"No, he likes tea," Frank said. "When he gets *burned*, he says things just to be contrary. A little *light* in the head, you know?"

Joe's eyes widened with a rush of comprehension, and he narrowed them again before Starkey saw. He finally understood what his brother was up to.

Frank poured his own tea while watching Mickey carefully. Mickey, a chain-smoker, drew a pack of cigarettes from his pocket with one hand, forcing a cigarette out with his thumb. He grasped it with his teeth and put the pack back. Then his hand went into another pocket and came out with a wooden match. All the time, he kept his eyes on Frank and Joe.

"Any lemon?" Frank asked. Mickey scratched the match head with his thumbnail, lighting it.

"This isn't a restaurant," Starkey said. "Drink up." Mickey raised the match to his lips.

"I *would* like some tea, Frank," Joe said. He sprang off his bed, moving toward Mickey with a teacup in his outstretched hand. Mickey kept the gun aimed at Joe.

Frank grabbed the teapot and threw the steaming water into Mickey's face. Mickey shrieked, one hand flying to his eyes, his pistol swinging toward Frank. Twisting out of the way, Frank clamped a hand on Mickey's wrist and pinched. The gun dropped out of his hand.

Joe caught the revolver in midair and turned it on Starkey while Frank smashed the teapot on Mickey's head. The gunman dropped to his knees, clawed at the air, and then plunged forward. The cigarette rolled from his lips and Frank ground it out underfoot.

"Out like a light," Frank said, looking down at Mickey.

"Your flunky should have known smoking was hazardous to his health," Joe told Starkey. Slowly Starkey's hand moved toward his coat. "Huh-uh," Joe said, wagging the gun up and down. "Hands where we can see them."

Starkey moved his hands out to the side and splayed his fingers. Joe seized Starkey's shoulder, spun him around, and slammed him against the wall.

"The shoe's on the other foot, pal," Joe said. He jabbed the revolver's muzzle into Starkey's spine.

Frank frisked Starkey. He had a forty-five in a coat pocket, plus a thirty-eight special in a holster on the back of his belt. Frank took them. "What my brother's trying to say is that the three of us are marching out of here. Together. You're going to lead us right past all your men."

"You cross me, you cross the United States government," Starkey said angrily. "You'll never be safe anywhere—"

"Shut up!" Joe barked. Roughly, he shoved Starkey to the door. "Move."

Frank reached the door first and looked down the hall. There was no one. "Looks like your men aren't staying as close as you thought." He pulled Starkey out of the door. "We'll give you a better deal than you gave us. Just play along until we're outside, and you'll come out of this in one piece."

"But remember who has the guns," Joe said.

At a normal pace they walked down the hall and rounded a corner. On a chair next to the bank of elevators, a balding man in a business suit was seated, reading a newspaper. He was overweight, and his extra bulk pushed the outline of a gun and shoulder holster into his coat. A walkie-talkie hung from his belt.

"One of yours, right?" Joe asked Starkey. Starkey said nothing, but his gritted teeth were answer enough. "Be cool."

The seated man looked up with a big grin as they approached. "Hey, Starkey," he said cheerfully. "What gives? Thought you were working late tonight."

With a wink and a smile, Starkey said, "You know what they say about all work and no play."

Frank hit the elevator button and waited impatiently for the elevator to arrive. Joe stood a few feet behind Starkey as Starkey and the seated man chatted on. It was meaningless talk about the weather in San Francisco. Frank almost laughed. He had no idea Starkey had such trivial talk in him.

At last the bell chimed and the elevator doors slid open. As they moved into the elevator, Starkey cried, "Trouble, Charlie. Move!"

With dazzling speed, the man on the chair drew his pistol. His jovial smile warped into a no-nonsense frown. "Everyone out of there. Now!"

Starkey blocked the elevator doors with his body. "Good work, Charlie." He reached back to grab at Frank.

Joe kicked Starkey forward, knocking him into the hall. The agent in the hall opened fire and the boys ducked to either side as the elevator doors slid shut. The elevator began its descent.

"How are we going to get out of here, Frank?" Joe asked. "Starkey's men will be all over the lobby." He stared at the gun in his hand and finally put it in his pocket. "We can't shoot our way out."

"It's a good thing Starkey didn't know we wouldn't have gunned him down," Frank said. "As to getting out, I've been giving it some thought, and—"

The lights went out and the elevator jolted to a stop.

"It's Starkey," Joe said. "Remember the walkie-talkie on the other guy's belt? He probably called his men downstairs and had them override the elevator. We're trapped."

Abruptly, the lights came on. The elevator began to move again, but now it moved up. "He's reeling us in," Frank said. "We've got to stop this thing." He pushed the buttons for all the floors between them and Starkey.

The elevator passed the lit floors without pausing. The override was perfect. They couldn't stop it. With growing despair, Frank watched the number indicator flash with each floor they passed.

"Joe," he said, "I've got a plan."

Starkey stood ready as the elevator doors opened, his finger tense on the trigger of the gun he held. Doors fully open, he lunged into the elevator.

"They're not here!" he screamed in rage.

"That's impossible!" the balding man said. "The elevator didn't stop, so they couldn't have gotten off. How did they get out?"

"I don't know," Starkey snarled. He let the doors close again. "Get Mickey out of the room to help. I want every available man checking all the floors between here and the lobby. I'll get them yet."

He pounded on the elevator call button until another elevator came. "I'll see you downstairs," he called to the balding agent and left.

Two floors down, the door of the first elevator opened. Frank poked his head out and looked around. "It's safe, Joe. You can come down now."

Joe dropped through the emergency hatch at the top of the elevator. "Great idea, Frank. Hiding on top of the elevator car bought us some time, at least. Now where do we go?"

"To the last place Starkey would expect us to hide," Frank said. "Come on." He opened a window and climbed onto the fire escape. "Starkey's men will make travel through the halls difficult. We'd better take the scenic route."

They climbed the fire escape for two flights until they came to their room. "Shhh," Frank warned. "Mickey might be coming to right about now."

"I hope not," Joe said. He tried one window and then another. The second raised easily, and Frank and Joe climbed into the room. "Looks like they dragged him out. We're safe."

"As long as Starkey doesn't decide to come back, anyway," Frank said. "We better shower up while we have the chance. You want anything from room service?"

"A steak dinner. I'm famished," Joe said. "But won't that tip Starkey we're here?"

"I'll run that risk for a meal," Frank replied. He called the hotel kitchen and placed an order, then sank back onto the bed for a fitful nap while Joe took a shower.

A knock on the door woke him. "Room service," called a youthful voice from outside.

"I'm not really dressed!" Frank yelled back. "You better let yourself in." If it was really room service, Frank knew, that wouldn't be a problem. If it was Starkey's men, then Frank would have the better defensive position if he stayed away from the door.

Keys jingled in the door, and Frank squeezed the handle of Starkey's snub-nosed revolver, ready for trouble. Then he saw it. Starkey hadn't left the room unguarded after all. As the door began to swing open, a wire taped to the door at foot level tightened. On one end of the wire was enough thermite to turn the room to fine powder. All that was needed to trigger it was someone coming in or out of the room.

"No!" Frank screamed as the door swung open and the wire pulled taut.

Chapter

11

FRANK LEAPT FOR the door and slid across the rug. Just before the trip wire stretched to full tension, he ripped it from the door.

He quickly studied the bomb and realized his guess was correct. So long as the wire wasn't pulled completely taut, the bomb wouldn't ignite. Relieved, he rolled on his back, sprawling across the rug. He found himself staring up at the puzzled bellhop, who carried a tray full of food.

"Don't mind me," Frank said. "Put it anywhere." As the bellhop set the tray on the foot of the bed, Frank stood and dug his wallet from his pocket. His fingers brushed the crumpled plans to the Carlyle Museum, and he pulled out the paper and threw it on his pillow. The bellhop handed him the check.

"You can sign for your meal, sir," the bellhop

said. He still watched Frank suspiciously, but Frank smiled mischievously and took the check and pen. With a flourish, he put his signature on the check and handed it back.

"Can your tip go on that, too?" he asked.

"Yes, sir," the bellhop said.

"Write yourself in for a fifty-percent tip," Frank said. "I don't think we'll be needing anything else tonight."

"Yes, *sir!*" the bellhop said. The money had driven any doubts from the bellhop's mind. With a slight bow, he left the room, closing the door behind him. Frank turned the safety bolt. If anyone wanted to get in then, they'd have to break down the door to do it.

"Is it soup yet?" Joe called from the shower. He appeared in the bathroom door, a towel wrapped around him.

"Yeah, dinner's here," Frank replied. "And that's not all. Look." He bent over and picked up the thermite bomb.

Joe's jaw dropped. "Starkey?"

Frank nodded. "A little present, set to fry us and half this hotel."

"I can see playing for keeps in the espionage racket, but this guy's out of his mind," Joe said. "We've got to put him out of business, Frank, before someone really gets hurt."

Frank threw himself on the bed and took the lid off one of the plates on the food tray. The aroma of steak and baked potato hit his nostrils, and he inhaled deeply. "I already got a small shot back at him. He's paying for the room, remember? I ordered the most expensive meals and gave the bellhop a whopping tip. I'd like to see Starkey explain *that* on his budget reports."

They both laughed. "I guess we'd better get some sleep and find a new hotel in the morning."

For the first time Frank realized how tired he was. After they finished their meal, Joe took the first watch while Frank slept. He had no dreams, and no one else came to the room.

They were out of the hotel at seven the next morning. None of Starkey's men were anywhere around. It was as if the government man and his agents had never existed.

Half a mile away the Hardys checked into another hotel. At the coffee shop in the lobby, they were eating breakfast when, in the middle of a bite of toast, Joe asked, "Any ideas on what we do now?"

"Let's see where we are," said Frank, wiping his lips. "We've got Russians who've kidnapped Uncle Hugh to steal a crown for them. We've got a crazed counterespionage agent who's determined to prove Uncle Hugh's a traitor. And we've got some mystery woman—it's anybody's guess whose side she's on. We're stuck in a city three thousand miles from home, and we're being hunted by a government agency that has orders to shoot to kill.''

Joe grimaced. "Do you get the feeling we're out of our depth?"

"That's putting it mildly," Frank said. "The question is, what do we do about it? We've got to get more information."

"I vote we get it from Starkey," said Joe. "I'm itching to take a crack at him, just him and me. I know I can make him talk."

"Yeah, he seems to be at the center of this, more than Uncle Hugh and what's her name—Charity? From the way Starkey's been acting, I know he has more up his sleeve than he's been telling. Of course, we do know where Uncle Hugh and Charity live, but we haven't the faintest idea where to find Starkey."

"What did he say his agency's cover was?" Joe asked. "Transmutual Indemnity?"

"Yep," Frank said. "Same as Uncle Hugh's old company. Of course, he'll be at that office, and we know how to get there."

Joe grinned. "Let's stake out the place and wait for him to come out."

Frank chewed his lip, calculating the problems. "It'll be tricky. If we hang around too long, they'll see us. We can't afford to be spotted."

"Let's check in some yellow pages to see if there are any secondhand clothing stores around. And also the closest place we can buy charcoal."

At first Frank stared at his brother, puzzled.

Then, slowly, he smiled and went to get a phone book.

"I think that saleswoman wondered what we were up to," Joe said as he walked down Pine Street. He wore an oversize, crumpled suit with stains on it. A battered, floppy hat obscured his face, and two different shoes were on his feet. He tried to ignore the pain in his toes. He had carefully smeared charcoal over his face, giving the impression that he had neither shaved nor washed his face for days.

"We just should have told her we were going to be bums," Frank replied. He saw a modern concrete office building down the street. A bank was housed on the main floor, he knew, but an upper floor also contained the San Francisco offices of Transmutual Indemnity. "Good luck, and watch yourself."

They parted company at the street corner. Frank began to circle the block as Joe walked up to a trash can and began to paw through it. People walked near him as he dug, and wrinkling their noses, steered clear of him. Joe liked that. It made it easier for him to keep his eyes on the front door of the Transmutual office building.

By noon Frank had walked around the block a hundred times, and Joe had stretched on a lawn in front of a building across the street from Transmutual. He was pretending to be asleep, but one eye was open, watching everyone who moved on the street. People were swarming out of buildings, going to lunch. A tall, dark-haired man stood in front of the Transmutual building, glancing impatiently at his watch. I've seen him before, Joe thought, but try as he might he could not place him, and he dismissed the feeling.

At last the man called Mickey came out, his face a mask of rage. A few steps behind him was Starkey. Joe looked up, alarmed.

Frank had just rounded the far corner and was heading straight toward them. There was no warning Joe could give without blowing his own cover. Nervously he held his breath, watching Frank and waiting for the right moment to spring into action to rescue his brother.

To Joe's surprise, neither Mickey nor Starkey noticed as Frank walked by them. They were only interested in the dark-haired man. So, I should know him from somewhere, Joe realized. But he couldn't think of the name of the dark-haired man or where he knew him from.

Mickey turned abruptly and left, and Starkey and the dark-haired man strolled together down the block. They glanced in disgust at Frank and continued walking. When they were half a block on, Frank and Joe both followed, but separately.

At the corner Joe and Frank met. "That man," Frank whispered breathlessly. "You know who he is?"

"I've tried to place him, but couldn't," Joe admitted. "I'm sure I've seen him somewhere."

"You saw him in a limousine last night," Frank continued. "Picture him with a beard and an eye patch."

Joe blinked. "What? You mean—"

"It's Feodor," Frank said. "He's working with Starkey."

Chapter

12

"WAIT A MINUTE," Joe said. "Starkey working with the Russians? That doesn't make sense."

"I'm starting to think nothing does anymore," Frank said. "Every time I think I've got a handle on this business, some new wrinkle turns up. It's making me mad, Joe. When I think how people are playing games with Uncle Hugh's life—"

"We'll get to the bottom of it, Frank. One way or another." Joe kept his eyes on Starkey and Feodor. They walked up to an outdoor café and took seats at a table that looked onto the street.

Frank watched them carefully. Neither man looked as if he had been forced into this meeting. The pair chatted calmly, joking and laughing as the waiter took their order. They looked like old friends.

"I've got to hear what they're saying," Frank

said. Before Joe could stop him, he shambled across the street.

The restaurant's outdoor café almost jutted out onto the sidewalk, which was separated from the tables by a low, wrought-iron fence. Frank shuffled past table after table, slouching and hunching his shoulders, trying to keep his face hidden by his hat and collar.

"We're set for tomorrow night," Frank heard Feodor say without his Russian accent. As he wandered past their table, neither Starkey nor Feodor paid any attention to him. Feodor poured two glasses of wine, and he and Starkey each took one. "To success," Feodor said.

Starkey laughed. "To crime," he replied.

"Speaking of crime," Feodor began. Frank stood by the curb, parallel to their table, digging in trash that had collected in the gutter. From there, he could hear clearly.

Before Feodor continued, he shouted, "Hey, bum!"

For a moment Frank considered hurrying off. How had they discovered him? He had made certain he hadn't shown his face. Was it something in the way he moved? he wondered. The way he was dressed? Or perhaps, he thought, Starkey wanted something else. Crossing his fingers, he lowered his head so the hat cast a long shadow on his face, and he turned to face Feodor.

"You mind, pal?" Feodor asked. "Go mooch somewhere else, huh?"

Frank nodded, keeping his head down and slamming his fists into his pockets. He moved off. He had come away with just one bit of information. But, he thought, what a piece of info it is.

From behind him, Frank heard Starkey call, "Take a bath!" He turned to see Starkey and Feodor laughing at him.

Then Starkey took a narrow manila envelope from his pocket and slid it across the table to Feodor. The dark-haired man picked it up, slit it open, and began to leaf through the contents.

Suddenly Starkey's expression changed. He angrily grabbed Feodor's hand, forcing him to push the pieces of paper back into the envelope. Feodor's eyes flared and his voice rose, but Frank was now too far away to make out the words.

Starkey threw his napkin on the table and stormed away as Feodor continued to yell. At the corner Frank waited. When Starkey had passed him, he wandered back toward the restaurant. Feodor was still there, gleefully pulling the pieces of paper out again.

It was cash, Frank saw with a start. He moved by before Feodor saw him again, crossed the street, and hurried back to Joe.

"Money?" Joe asked when Frank told him what he had seen. "Think it's a shakedown?"

"No," Frank replied. They walked through San Francisco, discarding their secondhand clothes. "It was more like a payoff. They were all chummy until Feodor started counting the money there at the table. I think Starkey didn't want anyone to see it."

"Wow," Joe said. "Starkey having Russians on his payroll. Are we talking public or private payroll here?"

"I don't know," said Frank. "But there's something I do know, Joe. Feodor's not Russian."

"What?"

"Feodor's a fake. I heard him speak back there. He's as American as you or I."

"Are you sure he wasn't just putting it on to blend in?" Joe asked.

Frank shook his head. "Remember I told you his accent and his pal's kept shifting yesterday? This explains it. They're just *pretending* to be Russian."

Puzzled, Joe said, "No, it doesn't explain it. Uncle Hugh spent years behind the Iron Curtain. He'd know the difference between a real and a fake Russian accent, wouldn't he?"

"He's got to play along. They poisoned him," Frank said. "Joe, he's being set up for something. That's the only thing that makes sense."

"Then we've got to warn him," Joe decided.

"No," answered Frank. "We still don't have enough facts. If Uncle Hugh's seen with us, they might just finish him off on the spot. The trouble is, we're still on the edge of things. We've got to force the issue and make people bring the information we need to *us*. It's the only way we'll be able to piece things together before Uncle Hugh's time is up."

"Do you have anything in mind, brother?"

Frank nodded. "We steal the crown ourselves."

Joe glared at his brother in stunned disbelief. "You're joking."

"Why not?" Frank said. "We know what they're after and where it is. We have the plans on how to get to it, and we can pick up the supplies we need at any hardware store. That crown is what they want. We take it, and they'll have to come to us."

Joe rubbed his chin, thinking for a long time. Finally a smile drew up his mouth. "Frank," he said, "I like your thinking."

The Carlyle Museum stood on the edge of Golden Gate Park in a tree-lined yard with a gated entrance. Great stone steps led past Greek columns to the main building. Flat and two storied, it seemed out of place with the Greek columns that led up to it.

Out of place, Frank thought. Like everything else in this business. He was crouching in the bushes in the twilight, and for the hour he had been watching, no one had gone in or out of the museum. He was certain it was empty. Nervously, he fingered the rope he wore coiled around his waist, wishing Joe would hurry up.

"Boo," Joe whispered behind him, startling Frank. Suppressing a grin, Joe said, "Sorry I'm late. I decided to stop by the library and do some research. Did you get the stuff?"

Frank held up a knapsack full of equipment and pointed to the rope. "What did you find out?"

"This is a private museum," Joe said. "It really isn't open to the public except on special occasions." Checking to see that no one was approaching, they dashed from the bushes to the gate, shimmied over it, and dropped flat onto their backs in the grass. As Frank checked to see if anyone had watched them, Joe continued. "The museum puts together cultural exhibits for the State Department. Exhibits are lent out to museums all over the world. Think that that has anything to do with anything?"

"Maybe," Frank said. "But we don't have time to wonder about it now. Let's go." They stood and crept carefully to the front door of the museum. The twilight was eerily quiet.

The lock on the door had a nine-key pad instead of a key-and-cylinder lock. "Just like the lock on Uncle Hugh's place," Frank said. "Only this one sounds an alarm as soon as you punch in the wrong combination." He opened the knapsack and pulled out a screwdriver, pliers, rubber gloves, and a length of copper wire. With the screwdriver, he carefully pried off the number one key and the number nine key, exposing the wire inside the lock. He scraped the wire with the pliers until metal showed through the plastic coating. Frank pulled on the rubber gloves, then took the copper wire and touched one end of it to the bare wire on the number one key and the other to the number nine key.

Sparks flew from the lock and showered the Hardys. The museum door swung open, but no alarm sounded. They went inside and shut the door behind them.

"That was easy," Joe said as they walked down the marble hall.

"It gets a lot harder from here on in," Frank said. He studied the plans of the museum. "I've got to admire Uncle Hugh's ingenuity. He was born to be a cat burglar."

At the end of the hall was an immense room filled with glass cases. The ceiling was high, and moonlight streamed in through a skylight. A sprinkler pipe stretched across the ceiling. In the middle of the room was the case they were looking for, but it was surrounded by railings, making it far out of reach.

"Watch the floor," Frank said. "It's pressure sensitive. Our weight will touch off alarms if we step on it." He pulled the rope from his waist, unwound it, and threw one end high into the air.

It struck the sprinkler pipe, but instead of looping over it, it fell back to the floor. Frank groaned and waited for the alarms to sound.

All was quiet. The rope wasn't heavy enough to trip the alarm. Frank reeled it in and tossed it into the air again. This time, it fell over the pipe and dangled down. Slowly Frank fed it slack until it hung almost to the floor. Then he grabbed the end, tied it into a slipknot around the other end, and pulled the new loop tight around the pipe. It held.

He climbed the rope until he reached the pipe. Joe followed him up, and they moved hand over hand down the length of the pipe.

Suddenly Frank froze. Someone was walking down the hall.

"Starkey!" Joe whispered as a figure appeared in the darkened doorway. "What's he doing here?"

"Shhh," Frank said. "I'm more worried about Mickey." The other man had appeared next to Starkey, and Starkey turned away from the door to talk to him.

"Any progress with our loose ends?" Starkey asked.

They're talking about us, Frank realized. Just great.

"We found their new hotel, but they haven't come back yet," Mickey said. "We'll get them."

"I don't want them fouling up my plans for Hunt," Starkey warned. "Shoot on sight, and shoot to kill."

We're sitting ducks up here, Frank thought. We're only safe as long as he doesn't look up. Then he saw the rope, dangling to the floor.

"Joe," he hissed. "The rope!"

Desperately, Joe swung hand over hand down the pipe, racing to get to the rope and pull it out of sight before Starkey saw it and discovered them. If that happened, they were dead.

As the Hardys dangled helplessly, Starkey slowly turned toward the rope.

Chapter

13

"MR. STARKEY," MICKEY CALLED.

With an exasperated sigh, Starkey spun on his heel to face Mickey, impatiently snapping, "What?"

Hanging on to the pipe with one hand, Joe reached out and snagged the rope. He pulled it up, looping it over the pipe to keep it from falling again.

"Ted says he thinks Hunt is going to pull something," Mickey said. "I told you he was too dangerous and clever to play around with."

"I don't want you calling Ted anything but Feodor until this operation is over," Starkey said coldly. "Let Hunt try anything, and he can just curl up and die in"—he glanced at his watch—"just a few hours." Starkey stepped into the exhibit room. To Frank's surprise, no alarms sounded.

He switched them off, Frank realized. It made sense. If Starkey had some connection with the museum, he would make sure he could trip no alarms. They probably wouldn't be reset until he and Mickey left. All the effort he and Joe wasted to break in, and they could have just walked in the door.

Starkey walked to the crown case, spreading his arms out to rest his hands on either side of it. Leaning forward, he stared at the golden crown. "Yes, sir," he said. "This little baby and Hugh Hunt are going to end all our problems."

Mickey shook his head in disgust. "It's a mistake. Hunt is a tiger. There's nothing more dangerous than a wounded tiger."

"He's nothing," Starkey snapped. "He's a peregrine, and I shot him out of the sky." Angrily he stormed from the room. With a shrug, Mickey took a quick look at the golden crown, then followed Starkey out.

Joe dropped the loose end of the rope to the floor and slid down it. He swung the rope over to Frank, who eagerly grabbed it. Once on the floor, he massaged his sore shoulders and fingers.

"It's about time they left," Frank said. "I didn't know how much longer I could hang on."

"Did you hear him?" Joe said excitedly. "The alarms are off. This is our chance."

"Right," Frank agreed. They stepped over to the crown exhibit, and he drew a glass cutter and a suction cup from the knapsack.

"That's it?" Joe said. "That's what all the fuss is about?" He studied the crown. It was much smaller than he had expected and less ornate. But what made it interesting was that it appeared to have been made of a single thread of gold, woven back and forth.

"Disappointed?" Frank asked. He licked his fingers and ran them over the rim of the suction cup, then pressed the moistened cup onto the top of the glass case.

"It looked better on film," Joe said. "The photos must have been blown up." He watched as Frank dragged the blade of the glass cutter in a rough circle around the suction cup. Metal met glass with a high-pitched scratching that echoed through the quiet museum. Joe looked over to the door, ready for trouble. But Starkey had not heard the noise.

"Here goes nothing," Frank said. He twisted the suction cup, and there was a creak of glass on glass. Then he pulled up, and the glass circle came up with the suction cup.

Eyes bright, Joe reached into the case and grabbed the crown. "This was so easy I think Starkey *wants* it stolen."

"I'm pretty sure he does," said Frank. But not by us, he thought. He set the glass and cup on the case, and Joe handed him the crown. Frank held it up to the dim moonlight that came in from above. The yellow metal seemed to glow, diffusing the light into a golden haze. The crown felt warm in his hand.

"You've got that look on your face," Joe said. "What's bothering you?"

"There's something wrong here," Frank said. He dropped the crown into the knapsack and zipped it closed. "Let's talk about it when we're outside."

They dashed from the exhibit room and ran down the long hall to the front door. Starkey and Mickey were nowhere to be seen.

At the front door Frank halted abruptly in his tracks. "We can't leave yet," he told his brother.

Joe stared at him. "Are you kidding? We've got two killers wandering around in here. They'd just as soon shoot us as talk to us. We've got the crown. What are we waiting for?"

"The crown is a bargaining chip," Frank said. "But we don't know why. What are Starkey and Mickey doing here? You said this place is run by the State Department and helps to put together cultural exhibits. Did you happen to notice where the exhibits were sent?"

"Germany, Singapore, South Africa, places like that," Joe said.

"No Soviet bloc nations?" Frank asked.

"Not that I noticed," Joe said. "What are you getting at?"

Frank sighed. "I don't know. It was starting to seem like this place was a front for Starkey's agency—"

"That would explain how Starkey got in so easily."

"But it doesn't explain what Espionage Resources uses the place for," Frank continued. "If they sent exhibits to Communist countries, agents could go along as curators. But they don't, so that blows that theory."

He unfolded his map of the museum, ran his finger over it, and stopped where a door was marked. "Here's the office. I want to check there for records on this exhibit. If we can figure out where it's going, maybe we can figure out why the crown is so important. Then we'll really have something to bargain with."

Joe shrugged. He wanted to leave, but he knew better than to try to change his brother's mind. "Lead on," he said, and, as if to comfort himself, added, "Maybe I'll finally get a crack at Starkey."

Cautiously, they walked through the corridors. After several wrong turns, Frank stopped and studied the map. "If I've got this figured right," he said, "the office will be right around this corner."

Joe noticed a metal box on the wall and swung

the door of the box open. "I think you're right this time, brother. These are the controls for the alarm system. They wouldn't have them far from the office, would they?"

Without answering, Frank turned the corner. At the end of the corridor was a door, the word *Curator* written on its opaque window. Above it was another small box with lights.

Frank recognized it as an alarm indicator. The alarm was still off. He turned the knob on the door and found it locked. With the glass cutter, he made a small arc at the corner of the window in the door.

Wrapping his hand in his jacket, he pushed in the pie-shaped piece of glass. It fell away where Frank had cut it and smashed delicately to the floor. White in the face, Joe frantically rounded the corner. "What was that noise?"

Frank reached through the break, unlocked the door from the inside, and entered the room. "Don't worry about it," he told Joe. "You'd better stand guard in the hall."

Nodding, Joe vanished around the corner again. Frank looked the room over. On the opposite wall it had another door, leading to the outside. A desk sat at one end of the room, and Frank switched on a small lamp on top of it. In the soft glow he saw metal file cabinets lined against a wall, and he went to them. Pressing his hands against the cool metal, Frank leaned against the cabinets and studied the labels. "Pre-

Columbian Jewelry," he read, pulling one drawer open. To his relief, it was not locked.

In seconds he found the file he was looking for and took it to the desk. He flipped through it until he found the tour schedule. It was for an Asian tour; the artifacts would be sent to Japan, South Korea, Hong Kong, and Malaysia. There was nothing that would help him. He was still as in the dark as ever.

As he was closing the file, a scrap of paper fluttered out. He picked it up and read it with interest.

The crown had needed some small repair, it said, and the work delayed the exhibit by three months. The signature on the repair authorization belonged to W. B. Starkey.

He returned the scrap to the file, and the file to the drawer. The drawer had just slid shut when the knob on the door to the outside began to turn. In a flash Frank lunged to the desk and switched off the lamp, and as the outside door swung open, he ran into the hallway.

Frank had barely gotten ten feet when a chilling voice behind him said, "Freeze." Frank stopped.

"Raise them high and turn around slowly," Starkey said. Frank lifted his hands and the knapsack over his head, and turned.

"I knew you'd come here tonight," Starkey continued, and though Frank couldn't see his face, he could imagine the smirk on it.

Where was Joe? he wondered. He hoped his

brother had gotten away. Light from under the hall door glinted off the gun in Starkey's hand, and Frank knew what was in store for him.

"You've lost," Starkey said. "And I've won. Time to say bye-bye." He switched on the overhead light and took aim.

Chapter

14

"You!" Starkey sputtered. "But where— It was supposed to be— What are you—"

He shut his mouth, opened it again as if he were going to say something, then closed it. Rage and frustration danced across his face. His eyes narrowed into slits as he stared at Frank. Slowly he regained his composure, the gun still aimed at Frank.

Frank said nothing.

Finally, Starkey said, "Where is he?"

"I don't know where my brother is," answered Frank.

"Who cares about your brother?" Starkey exploded. "You weren't supposed to be here tonight, neither of you. Hugh Hunt was. Who told you about this place?"

Frank smiled. Feodor and Oleg didn't tell him

115

they had lost the plans for the break-in. That made sense. He had seen Starkey in action, the blustery way he rode roughshod over Mickey. The fake Russians must have been too afraid to warn him about snags in his plan. For the first time Frank felt that he might have the upper hand.

Starkey cocked the revolver. "Answer me!"

"No one told me about it. It was only good detective work," Frank said. "I thought my uncle was supposed to steal the crown tomorrow night, not tonight."

Starkey swallowed hard, and Frank could see he had rattled him. "Hunt specializes in the unexpected. I thought he'd be here ahead of schedule. If he had stolen the crown, I could have gotten him for sure." Starkey curled his lip, spitting out the words. "You stole the crown, didn't you?"

Frank waved the knapsack. "I'll trade it to you for my life."

With a laugh that was more like a cough, Starkey said, "What's to stop me from gunning you down and just taking the crown, smart guy?" Before Frank could answer, he released the gun hammer and slowly lowered it back into place with his hand. "But I've got a better idea. Take the crown out very slowly and set it on the floor. Maybe I'll even let you live."

But you won't, Frank thought. He looked around for an out but saw none. The adjoining hall was too far behind him, and Starkey was too far ahead. He knew he could reach neither before Starkey shot him down.

"Come on, kid," Starkey said, taunting him. "I haven't got all night."

Frank's eyes opened wide for an instant as he watched the alarm light above Starkey's head go on. Starkey hadn't noticed it, even lit by the glow from the flashing red light, but Frank knew what the light meant—Joe had armed the alarm system.

"I'll get the crown," Frank said. "Just don't shoot me, please." He dug into the bag, and Starkey suddenly became alert, aiming even more carefully at Frank.

"Slowly," Starkey said.

Frank paced his movements. He pulled the crown from the bag, and Starkey's eyes brightened.

Frank threw the knapsack at Starkey's head as hard as he could. Starkey shot twice into the bag, and it fell to the floor like a wounded bird.

Frank disappeared around the corner.

"Are you all right?" Joe asked.

"Fine," Frank said, tossing the crown to his brother. "We've got about two seconds' lead on Starkey, so let's make the best of it. Back to the exhibit room."

"But if we go in there when the alarms are on, we'll be trapped," said Joe as they ran. A shot ricocheted off the wall.

Frank grabbed his arm and pulled him into a

doorway, out of the line of fire. Down the hall, Joe saw the exhibit room. All they had to do was get there.

"Now!" Frank whispered. They hurled themselves into the hall. Something roared behind them, and plaster from the wall above them sprayed into Frank's eyes. With Joe at his side, he slid across the tile floor and into the exhibit room.

Alarms blared and, as Frank knew it would, a shatterproof glass door slid closed, sealing off the room. They could see Starkey on the other side, pounding angrily on the glass, but the deafening ringing of the alarms drowned out his words. Over the din, Joe yelled, "Now what do we do?"

In his brother's ear, Frank said, "The cops will be all over this place in a few minutes. That should slow Starkey down some."

"But what about us?" Joe asked.

Frank smiled. "We're out of here. Follow me."

He walked to the rope and pulled on it once, testing it for strength. It was still tied securely to the sprinkler pipe. In seconds he had climbed up the rope, with Joe right behind him, his eyes fixed on the skylight above.

"Get ready to catch me," he said.

Carefully, he swung his feet up, caught his knees over the pipe, and pulled himself up. He reached out, but it was no use. The skylight was too far away. Balancing himself in place with his hands, Frank brought his feet up to the pipe and stood up on it.

He pressed a hand to the skylight to balance himself, and with the other hand took the glass cutter from his pocket. As hard as he could, he scraped a star into the glass.

The glass didn't break, but the cuts had been deep. Frank dropped the cutter to the floor. He slid an arm from his jacket and let the jacket drop behind his back. He slid the jacket from his other arm and caught it in his hand before it fell. Wrapping the jacket around his hand until it became a cloth lump, he struck the star on the glass with all his might.

It didn't shatter. He struck again. Still the glass stayed in one piece.

"Let a pro do it!" Joe yelled. He pulled himself up as Frank had done. He wobbled on the pipe until Frank caught his belt and steadied him. Joe handed Frank the crown and then took Frank's jacket and wrapped it around his hand.

He hauled his arm way back and let loose with a haymaker. The glass cracked. He hit it again, and it fell from the skylight frame in shards.

Joe knocked the remaining fragments of glass away from the frame and then pulled himself up. In seconds Frank was out, too. They stood on the roof, watching police cars approach the park.

"Let's move," Frank said, sliding his arm through the crown until it dangled like a bracelet.

Gazing at the trees in back of the building, he took a few steps back on the roof, built up to a full sprint, and leaped. His hands snatched out at a tree limb. Bark scraped into his hands, but his grip held. He was safe.

Gracefully, without a running start, Joe leapt. To Frank's horror, he missed the tree and plunged. But with a carefree laugh, Joe caught a lower branch and hung there. "You coming or what?" he asked Frank.

They climbed down to the ground, watching the red lights flash in front of the museum. "We'd better leave," Frank whispered. They ran through the park, staying off the street.

At Fulton Street they stopped running. Now that the danger was over, they were relieved, but their strength had left them.

"Let's take a cab the rest of the way," Joe said. "We deserve a rest."

"Sounds good to me," said Frank. He stood on the curb, waving his hand at the oncoming traffic. Two empty cabs passed them by. "I don't think this works like it does in New York, Joe. Maybe you have to call for cabs in this town."

"Let me try it." Joe pushed his brother aside and stuck out his hand. Another cab zipped by. "You know, we have to go to a new hotel again. Starkey knows where we're staying."

"I know," said Frank. He put out his hand again in a last-ditch effort to hail a cab.

To their surprise, a cab blinked off its top light

and pulled over to the curb. They climbed in and gave the driver a downtown address.

"I think I've figured this out," Frank said. "Starkey's trying to frame Uncle Hugh for some reason. So he created a couple of fake Russians who forced Uncle Hugh to work with them. And then Starkey was planning to catch Uncle Hugh in the act tonight."

"So he caught us instead," said Joe. "Swell." He took the crown from Frank and examined it.

"But I think the crown was just bait," Frank said. "In and of itself, the crown is worthless."

"Wrong," said a soft voice from the front seat. A woman sat up on the passenger side, a strawberry blonde with bright blue eyes. In her hand was a gun, and it was pointed straight at them. For the first time Joe looked at the driver. It was Kwan.

"Hi, Joe," Charity said. "Thanks for stealing the crown for me. It really is worth a great deal of money." She smiled, and Joe smiled back faintly. "You can hand it over now."

She held out her hand, and, reluctantly, Joe put the crown in her palm. "At last," she said. She squeezed her hand around it and twisted it in her fingers. Then her face reddened with anger.

"Fake," she cried, rage choking her voice. "It's a fake!"

Chapter

15

"WHERE IS IT?" asked Charity.

"Where's what?" Joe replied. "That's the crown we took. What you see is what you get."

Furious, she threw the crown in his face. "Feel it," she said. "Gold is cool to the touch. That isn't even metal. Now where's the real one?"

"Who *are* you?" Frank asked.

"Frank, this is Charity," said Joe. "Charity, Frank. She's the one I was telling you about."

"Ah. The one with the nice house and the photographs," Frank said. "I wish I could say I was pleased to meet you."

"We're wasting time," said Charity. "You have one more chance to keep this pleasant."

Frank sighed. "Joe's telling the truth. That one's all we've got." He could tell by the look in her eyes that she didn't believe him.

With a shrug, Charity waved the pistol in their faces. "Please sit still. I'd rather not shoot you." To Kwan, she said, "We'll get answers out of them at the house."

Kwan grinned and stepped on the gas, heading for Chinatown.

"Just so we're all clear on why we're here, let me give you a demonstration," Charity said.

Frank and Joe sat strapped back to back in chairs on the second floor of Charity's home. The room was lit by a single lamp, which cast huge shadows on the bare walls. Unlike the other floors, it was stripped of antiques, except for an old oil lamp suspended from the ceiling. Its seven metal cups had once held fuel oil, but now they were empty, waiting to be filled.

From a cabinet, Charity brought a glass vial that held a clear liquid. In her other hand, she held a small metal bowl on a ceramic dish. Setting the bowl and dish on the floor where the Hardys could see them, she poured several drops from the vial into the bowl. It sizzled and steamed where it struck metal. An acrid taste filled the Hardys' mouths as they inhaled the fumes.

"This is a special kind of acid used in antiquing furniture," Charity explained. "They dab it on wood to burn in scars and make the wood look old. As you can see, the acid ate through the metal bowl. But, of course, it has no effect on ceramics.

"Now," she said. "Let's begin again."

"Can I ask you a question first?" Frank asked.

Charity cocked her head and eyed him with suspicion. "I'd hardly be a proper hostess if I said no. What can I do for you?"

"Where do you fit in all this? Why do you want the crown?"

She smiled a little. "Discretion forbids me from telling any names, Frank, but there's an art collector in Italy who'll pay me six figures for that piece." She twirled the fake on her finger. "Not this piece of junk. The real one. Now, suppose you tell *me* something—"

"We've told you," Joe said. "We don't know."

"Kwan!" she called. The man came through the door, carrying a stepladder. He set it up next to Frank and Joe's chairs, took the vial from Charity, and climbed to the top of the ladder. Joe craned his neck to watch Kwan pour the acid into the lamp cups, but Frank kept his eyes on Charity.

She strolled to the window, opened it, and breathed in the salt air rolling in off the ocean. In the distance a church bell chimed midnight. "At quarter past," she said almost absentmindedly, "the acid will eat its way through the lamp and begin to drip. If it hits your face, you'll end up in bad shape. If it hits the top of your head, your condition will be much worse.

"I'd be happy to move you out of the way," Charity said sweetly. "If you'd just cooperate."

"We're as cooperative as possible," Frank said. "There's nothing more we can tell you."

"Save your breath, Frank," Joe said. "This dirty spy won't believe a thing we say."

"Spy!" Charity cried in outrage. "I've got scruples, brother. I'm a thief and nothing less. Spy! What a thing to say."

"I suppose Kwan isn't Red Chinese, then," Joe said accusingly.

At that, both Charity and Kwan roared with laughter. When the laughter died down, Kwan said, "I was born in Houston, and my family has lived in this country for one hundred and fifty years. Why on earth does he think we're spies, Charity?"

"Perhaps I can answer that," said a voice from the doorway.

Charity and Kwan spun to face a rugged, grinning man with white curly hair. A pistol glinted in his hand.

"Uncle Hugh!" Joe cried.

"Hello, Joe," he said. "What's the matter, Frank? Aren't you glad to see me?"

"The last time I saw you, you let two men drag me off to my death without lifting a finger to help," Frank replied.

Hugh Hunt swaggered into the room. His face was white, and Joe noticed his gun hand shaking slightly. He's sick, Joe thought. It's the poison getting to him.

"Not lift a finger?" their uncle said. "Who do

you think supplied the motorbike with which your brother rescued you?"

"You were the man in the helmet!" said Joe.

"Forgive me, Frank," his uncle continued. "But it was very important that I let Starkey think I was playing by his rules. Believe me when I say you were never in any real danger. I'd have stepped in to save you if I'd had to."

"That's very comforting," Frank said, but he didn't mean it.

Hugh stepped casually into the room and leaned against the door frame. "I must say I was surprised to see you involved in this business at all. How did Starkey con you into it?"

"We wanted to help you," Joe said. "And Starkey wanted us to help him investigate you."

"That's very interesting," Hugh said, with a sly grin. "Especially since I've been investigating him."

"What?" said Frank and Joe.

For a moment their uncle shivered and swayed. Brushing sweat from his brow, he steadied himself. "I'll explain some other time. Right now I need the crown for a trade. Where is it?"

"They haven't got it," Charity said. "And they claim they don't know where it is."

The news shook him. "But I watched them steal it."

Charity nodded. "Me, too. But all they came out with was this." She held up the crown. "A counterfeit. Not even gold."

"I know," said Hugh. "That's what I want." He stepped forward, stretching out his hand, but every step was a bit shakier.

"It's worthless," Joe said, bewildered. "You need the real one."

"That one's only worth thousands. This one's worth millions," his uncle explained. "To Starkey, anyway, and to our government." He neared Charity. "Hand it over."

"Sure," she said and reached out to drop the crown into his hand. At the last second she snatched it away. "Kwan!" she shouted, throwing it across the room.

Kwan caught the crown, and Hugh spun to aim at him. In that instant Charity kicked out, jabbing Hunt behind the knee with her heel. His legs buckled beneath him. He hit the floor with a loud thud, and the gun skidded from his hand.

Trying to gather his wits, Hugh crawled for his gun, but Kwan darted across the room and kicked the weapon out of his grasp. On his hands and knees, Hugh continued toward it, but Kwan barred his way to the weapon. The Chinese-American laughed as Hugh Hunt tried to pull himself up by grabbing Kwan's hand for support.

Suddenly Kwan's face twisted with pain. He sank to his knees as the boys' uncle rose up, his thumb and index finger pinching Kwan's hand. Thrilled, Joe realized his uncle had been faking his weakness to gain the advantage. Hugh shoved

Kwan away and snatched the crown from him as he fell.

Charity scrambled for her gun, but Hugh reached his first. He spun and fired.

The floor light shattered, plunging the room into darkness. In a flash Hugh was out the door with the crown. "Kwan!" Charity shouted angrily. "Get up! After him! I'm not passing up a chance at millions."

The Hardys heard Kwan groan, followed by the noise of the big man getting to his feet. Then came pounding footsteps as he followed Charity out.

"What about us?" Joe called after them. There was no answer but the slamming of the downstairs door, followed by silence. "What about us?" he muttered in desperation, although no one but Frank could hear.

With a sizzle, acid dripped past him, burning a scar in his chair.

Chapter

16

JOE STRAINED TO move his chair, but the old wooden frame was too heavy to budge. A drop of acid spattered and hissed on the floor. He looked up into the darkness. The metal of the lamp was starting to go. They had minutes, perhaps seconds, until the acid dissolved the lamp and came raining down on them. "I can't overturn the chair," he told Frank. "Maybe I can stand up."

"Don't waste your time," Frank said. "If you're tied like me, you don't have the leverage. Are your hands tied in back of the chair?"

"Yes."

"Good. Try to grab my hands," Frank ordered. They strained until their hands touched, and their fingers locked together. "I keep telling you, Joe. Leverage will get you out of situations where strength won't do any good. Singly, all we have is strength. Together, we have leverage. Push."

They leaned back until the backs of their chairs touched each other, and then, slowly, they forced the chair feet back, too. Pressed against each other, they stood. Acid spattered all around them now, spitting liquid fire on their clothes, but they ignored the pain.

"Right?" Joe asked.

"Right to you, left to me," Frank said. "One. Two. Three. *Shift*." At the same instant, they threw their weight to the sides of the chairs, pushing up with their feet.

The chairs toppled over, throwing them to the floor on their sides as acid poured down on the spot where they had sat seconds before.

"You all right?" Frank asked.

"I'll need a new pair of shoes," said Joe, glancing at the steam rising where the acid had splattered on his soles. "Now what?"

Frank let go of Joe's hands and started to work on Joe's ropes instead. "Now we try to untie each other before anyone gets back."

"Maybe I can be of some help." A light went on, and their uncle stood in the doorway again. His hand emerged from his pocket, holding a jackknife. "Sorry I took so long, but it took a few minutes to throw your lady friend and her assistant off my trail. I got back as soon as I could."

"Oh, we don't mind," Frank said, his voice tinged with sarcasm. "We managed to keep busy."

Hugh knelt and cut their ropes. "Honestly, Frank. If you can't get out of a little trap like this, you have no future in the business." There was laughter in his voice, but it faded as his eyes met Frank's stern gaze. More seriously, he said, "I suppose I owe you an explanation."

"True," Frank agreed. He stood, rubbing his wrists, as his uncle cut Joe free. "But it can wait until we get out of here."

"I can't give you one," Hugh continued as they ran for the stairs. "This is top security. You'll have to trust me."

Frank stopped abruptly, his eyes on a phone on a pedestal in the hall. He snatched the receiver from the cradle. "Talk to us or the cops. At this point it doesn't make much difference to me."

"No!" Hugh shouted. His hand slammed down on the cradle, cutting off the line. "All right. But it's a long story. Let's talk while we walk."

Frank nodded, and they left the house.

"Why didn't you ever tell us you were a spy?" asked Joe as they strolled toward their uncle's apartment.

Hugh laughed. "That's not the sort of thing you tell people, Joe. Especially not people you like. Have you told your parents about the work you've done for the Network?"

"He's got a point, Joe," Frank said. "Okay, Uncle Hugh, so you're a spy. It's not the past that concerns me, it's the present." He held up the crown and examined it. "Charity was right. This isn't gold." He ran his fingers over it. "It feels like some kind of glass, or plastic."

"You read computer and technical journals, Frank," his uncle replied. "I'm surprised you don't recognize the material."

"What could be so valuable that Starkey would go to all this trouble for it?" Frank snapped his fingers. "Of course. Fiber optics!"

"Fiber what?" Joe asked.

"They're used in communications, Joe," Hugh explained. "A vast improvement over wires and cables. This particular fiber is the next generation of fiber optics, one hundred times better than the batch in current use."

"So what's it doing in the shape of an Incan crown?" Frank asked. "No, let me guess. Starkey, or one of his agents, stole the fiber from the laboratory where it was being developed."

"Right," said his uncle Hugh. "And Espionage Resources was brought in to investigate, so he covered his own tracks. He's worked that way to steal American technology before. That's what tipped us off to him."

"Us?" Joe said. "I thought you were retired."

"I was," he said. "But I was asked back. They needed someone who knew the organization, someone whom Starkey wouldn't expect."

"So Starkey arranges the State Department-sponsored art exhibits through the Carlyle Museum," Frank continued. "He dummies up what he steals to look like artifacts or art, and gets things out of the country that way."

"As near as I can figure it," said his uncle, "the objects are then 'stolen' on tour by the people he's selling to."

"So everyone thinks that art is being stolen, not technology?" Joe asked as they approached Hugh's building.

Hugh nodded. "And low-grade art, at that. Low priority. No one's ever that interested in tracking it down. It's cheaper just to write it off."

"And the real art?"

"As near as I can figure, it ends up in Starkey's private collection." Hugh's voice tapered off, and his breath became uneven. Suddenly he pitched forward, nearly losing his footing. Frank caught him and kept him from falling. "Poison. Starting to eat through me. I'll be all right, though. Get me upstairs."

Quickly they carried him through the front door and into the elevator. When they reached the condominium, the Hardys stretched their uncle Hugh out on the living room sofa. After a few moments the color began to flow back into his cheeks.

"We've got to find Starkey and force him to give you the antidote," Joe said, but his uncle raised a hand to silence him. He reached for a cordless phone on the coffee table in front of the couch.

Hugh pulled up the antenna and punched in the phone buttons. After a moment the phone clicked. "Starkey? I've got something you want, and you've got something I want. Let's meet." Starkey's voice was muffled, and neither Joe nor Frank could make out the words. "I know the place. See you on the Embarcadero in an hour."

Hugh pressed the antenna back into the handset and hung up the phone. "We've got a lot of work to do," he said. "I'm going to wire myself and try to tape Starkey admitting to everything. One of you will have to hold the recorder." His hands shook, but there was resolve in his eye. He went to his desk, opened it, and pulled out a small radio-microphone and some surgical tape. Pulling off his shirt, he fastened the mike to his chest.

"This is too dangerous," Frank said. "Starkey will take the crown and leave you to die. I can't go along with this plan."

Smiling, Hugh told Joe, "I guess that makes you my sound engineer." Hugh dug a small tape recorder from the drawer and handed it to Joe. "There are some keys in a jar on the bookshelves, Frank."

"I know. I found them before," Frank said. "What are they for?"

"A car in the garage around the corner," his uncle replied. His hands shook as he put his shirt back on. To Frank's surprise, the wire didn't show beneath the shirt. "Why don't you bring it around? Stall one fifty-three."

Frank glowered at him and said nothing. "Come on, Frank," Hugh pleaded in the same kidding way he had once nudged Frank to go fishing when Frank was a boy. "Play along with me."

Shaking his head doubtfully, Frank took the keys and left.

Hugh picked up the crown and slipped it into his pocket, then winced and grabbed at his side. Joe moved to help him stand, but his uncle waved him away and straightened himself.

"I don't think you can do this," Joe said.

"I've got to," he answered. All humor was gone from his voice by then. "My life depends on it."

Joe stared at him for a long time. Finally he pocketed the recorder. "Then we'd better get going." Hugh clapped him on the back in appreciation, and together they went to the elevator.

"Well, well," called a mocking voice behind them as they stepped onto the street. "Fancy meeting you here."

Starkey was leaning against the limousine, his elbows propped casually behind him on the roof. Inside the limo sat Oleg, Feodor, and Mickey. All of them held guns, and all the guns were aimed at Joe and Hugh.

"How did you—?" Hugh stammered in surprise. "I just called you at your office."

"You've never heard of a car phone?" Starkey

said. "I've been sitting around the corner since the robbery, waiting for your call." Suddenly his eyes grew dark. "I've always been one step ahead of you, Hunt. And now it looks like you're all out of steps."

He moved over to Hunt and patted him down. When his hand hit the mike, his face grew dark, and he tore open Hugh's shirt and ripped the microphone from his chest. It fell to the pavement, and he ground it under his heel.

"Enough tricks. Where's the crown?" he demanded.

Somberly, Hugh pulled the crown from his pocket and handed it to Starkey.

"Where's your brother?" Starkey asked Joe.

Joe shook his head. "I don't know."

"It doesn't matter. We'll deal with him later," Starkey said. He opened the limo door. "In."

As he and his uncle climbed into the limousine, Joe glanced down the street, looking for Frank and the other car. If he sees us, Joe thought, we've still got a chance.

"Don't even think it," Starkey said, noticing the hope on Joe's face. "Your chances are all used up."

He slammed the door. Then clenching his hand around the crown and grinning triumphantly, he got into the front seat, and the limousine drove off.

Chapter
17

THE EMBARCADERO STRETCHED along the water-front of San Francisco, from Fisherman's Wharf to the Oakland Bay Bridge. It was a neighborhood filled with docks and warehouses. A particularly seedy warehouse was the limousine's destination. Two men appeared from the shadows to slam the warehouse doors shut after the limo was safely inside.

Mickey got out of the car, opened the back door, and escorted Joe and Hugh Hunt out. To Joe, the warehouse looked immense, although he did know the shadows of the crates made it appear larger than it was.

"The Carlyle Museum's warehouse," Hugh said with a note of grudging admiration. "I figured you'd be using it, too."

"You've been out of the business quite a while,

Hunt. How is it you know so much about my operation?" Starkey asked as he, too, stepped out of the limousine. Feodor and Oleg followed him.

"You mean you don't know?" Joe blurted out in amazement.

Starkey's eyes narrowed. "Know what?"

Joe wanted to kick himself, but he saw he had snagged Starkey's curiosity, and he could use that to keep himself and his uncle alive, at least for a few more minutes. "Nothing," he said. "What I want to know is why you picked on my uncle."

"I had my reasons," Starkey said, smirking. "Now that you're not wired, I suppose there's no reason to keep it from you. I picked him because he's Hugh Hunt."

"That's not much of a reason," Joe said, all at once wondering why Starkey hadn't bothered to tie them up. But then, scanning the warehouse, the reason was obvious. He counted ten armed men in addition to Starkey, Mickey, and the two fake Russians.

"You've never had to live with it!" Starkey angrily exploded. "The man's a living legend in espionage. His shadow hung over us the whole time I was in training and in the field. 'This is how Hugh Hunt would have handled it,' they'd say. 'That's how Hugh Hunt would have handled that.' Well, look at him now. I've handled *you*, Hunt. I've killed your reputation and I'll take your life, and I'll finally wipe out your shadow for good."

"Jealousy," Hunt said in an unconcerned voice that made Starkey's eyes flare with rage. "You had a good little scam going here, Starkey. All you had to do was get that crown out of the country, and no one would have been the wiser. Why risk such a cozy setup just to get me?"

"You? You're nothing," Starkey replied. "I did it to save *me*. Espionage Resources is being investigated. I couldn't afford to get caught with the crown, and it wasn't time to get it out of the country."

"So you disguised your cronies," Hugh said, pointing at Feodor and Oleg, "as Russians, and made it look as if I'm working for them. I steal the crown, you catch me, and you kill me for resisting, right?"

Slowly Starkey nodded.

"Then you get the fiber optic wire back, you're a big hero because you smashed a smuggling ring, and I'm a clay hero who turned rotten."

"That's how it would have gone down, if it hadn't been for him and his brother," Starkey said, glaring at Joe. "But I can still pull it off. I've got tapes of your little friends linking you with the Russians."

"But there aren't any Russians!" Joe objected.

"There are people in Washington who think there are Russians everywhere," said Starkey.

"But it still won't work," Hugh said. "What

about your clients? They might get a little cross about not getting their merchandise."

"The crown can be lost during the arrest," Starkey said with a shrug. "Your body will be enough to take the heat off me. I'll just lie low for a while, and then it can be business as usual."

"Except for one thing," said Hunt. "I still have some friends in the espionage community, and they're on to you. They hired a special investigator." He sat casually on a crate. "Know who they sent to get the goods on you, Starkey?"

"Do tell," Starkey said. His eyes were twinkling because he thought Hugh was bluffing. "Who?"

"Me."

Starkey's eyes widened slowly, filled with despair. His lips opened and closed, but only a soft moan came out.

Joe peered into the shadows. Now his uncle had angered Starkey too much. The government agent had no reason now to keep them alive. Somewhere, he knew, there must be a way out. But everywhere he looked, armed figures loomed in the darkness, on the floor and even on the catwalks.

He blinked. At the back of the warehouse, one of the figures suddenly fell over. When the figure stood up, it was shorter and thinner than before. Slowly it grew larger, and Joe realized it was moving toward the front of the warehouse. But then he got distracted.

Starkey started screaming obscenities at the top of his voice. Mickey stared at his boss with horror. Starkey screamed until his throat would take no more. Then he just stood still, shaking, his face red with rage. "Mr. Starkey!" Mickey cried. "What does it matter?"

"It's no good," Starkey said as if he were explaining something to an idiot. "They sent him, don't you see? If we kill him, they'll swarm all over us. They won't buy a frame, not for a minute." Rubbing his forefinger back and forth across his mouth, he began pacing.

Joe watched the shadowy figure glide through the darkness, approaching another of Starkey's guards. Somewhere in the distance, he heard a buzzing, but paid no attention to it.

"I've got nothing to lose now," Starkey said, stopping in front of Hunt, whose breathing had become extremely labored. "They'll come after me sooner or later. But in the meantime, I'm going to have the pleasure of watching you die."

Hugh coughed. "It's going to be a long wait. I'm not due until tomorrow night."

Starkey roared with laughter. "I've been one step ahead of you all through this game. I knew you'd steal the crown ahead of time, so I had my men tell you the poison worked in about three days."

He smiled grimly. "It really works in a little more than two. You've got approximately a half hour."

"No!" Joe cried. He lunged at Starkey. A pistol butt cracked down on his skull, and he fell and rolled. He lay on the warehouse floor, staring up the barrel of Feodor's gun. The buzz grew into a dull rumble.

Starkey fished a small vial from his coat and held it up to the light bulb that dangled from the rafters. "You want this, Hunt? It's the antidote. I want you to die knowing your cure was six feet away, and you couldn't get to it."

Hugh staggered off the crate and swung at Starkey, who easily backed away. The older man sank weakly to his knees, and his hands dragged on the floor.

Taunting him, Starkey dangled the antidote. "You'll never taste it," he said. "Never."

"Yes, he will," said a voice from the back of the warehouse. Frank Hardy stepped out of the darkness, and, with the click of a safety being switched off, lowered an automatic rifle at Starkey.

"You really are sloppy, Starkey," Frank said. "A child could have followed your car. You should drive something nondescript."

"Maybe I wanted you to follow me," Starkey said. "I knew you were out there somewhere, and now I have all the 'loose ends' together."

Frank smiled. "But I have the gun."

"Ah," said Starkey. "But I've got you outnumbered." Frank flicked his eyes from side to side. A dozen guns were aimed at him. Starkey raised a hand and pressed his thumb and middle finger together. "All I have to do is snap my fingers, and you're history. I'll give you to the count of three."

Frank stared at him and didn't lower the gun.

"One," Starkey said.

Frank said nothing. The rumble sounded like thunder now.

"Two."

Why doesn't he drop it? Joe wondered. He knows there's no chance. But his brother stood firm. The rumble became a roar.

"Three!" Starkey shouted, and fingers throughout the warehouse tightened on triggers.

A dozen motorcycles crashed through the warehouse doors. The black-leather-clad riders were Chinese.

It was Charity's gang, led by Tony.

Joe kicked his foot out, catching Feodor in the ankle. As Starkey's man cried out in pain, Joe's hand shot to his wrist, catching it and tugging Feodor forward. Feodor dropped as Joe's fist hammered into his jaw. He collapsed in a lump.

The cycles roared around Starkey's agents, the riders swinging tire chains into the startled gunmen, who fired without taking aim. Frank swung his elbow up and brought it back hard into Mickey's stomach. Stunned, Mickey flailed out, and Frank stepped into the swing and grabbed Mickey's hand and elbow.

Continuing the spin, Frank brought his shoulder up into Mickey's chest and jerked forward. Mickey flew over Frank and crashed to a halt on Oleg. Frank took a karate stance and prepared for a counterattack, but neither man stirred.

"Frank!" Joe shouted over the din. "Where did the cycle hoods come from?"

"I took a moment to call Charity," Frank shouted back. "Remember when I threatened to call the police? I noticed her number on the phone then. I thought she might want to know where the real crown might be. Just a little bit of insurance I cooked up." He gazed at the melee. In the midst of it, Hugh was curled up on the floor, breathing hard and clutching at his stomach. Starkey was nowhere to be seen. In the chaos he had slipped away.

Joe gazed around as he knocked aside a man who charged at him. "I get the feeling someone's missing here, Frank. You seen Starkey around in the last couple minutes?"

"There he is!" Frank pointed at a figure sprinting to the back of the warehouse. Starkey came to a door, threw open a bolt, and dashed out.

The Hardys followed him outside. Behind the warehouse was a small pier, and at the end of the pier a motorboat was moored. Starkey was halfway down the pier.

"Freeze, Starkey!" Frank called out. To his surprise, Starkey stopped dead in his tracks. Turning to face Frank and Joe, Starkey spread his arms all the way out to the sides.

"You got me," he said. "And I've got you." In his right hand was the antidote, and he held it out over the water.

"Either I get in that boat and you let me get away," Starkey said, "or the antidote goes into the bay, and you never find it." He smirked confidently. "Well? Me or your uncle's life, which is it going to be?"

Chapter

18

"I'LL TAKE THAT bottle," said Charity. She rose up the ladder from the boat and stepped onto the pier behind Starkey.

Shrieking, Starkey stepped back and spun around, striking Charity with his fist, knocking her off balance before she could get her footing. Her feet twisted beneath her, and she toppled off the pier.

"I've had enough," Joe grumbled and hurled himself at Starkey.

"No!" shouted Frank, but it was too late. Joe smashed into Starkey with a flying body tackle. Starkey kicked out, shoving Joe aside. But Joe grabbed his leg as he tried to crawl to his feet. Starkey hammered at Joe's head and shoulders.

Joe slammed his fist into Starkey's stomach. Gasping for breath, Starkey fell away, and Joe flipped forward, pinning Starkey to the pier. Though Starkey bucked, Joe held him down. Slowly Joe's fingers crawled along his arm, reaching for the vial in Starkey's hand.

"We've got him," said Frank, standing over them. He reached for the vial. Too late he saw the malice in Starkey's eyes.

Starkey dropped the vial and tapped it hard with his finger before Joe or Frank could stop him. The vial rolled down the pier. Frank leaped to grab it.

Before his fingers could close around it, the vial vanished off the end of the pier and plunged into the water.

Angrily, Joe socked Starkey on the jaw to knock him out. The secret agent went limp and still. Under other circumstances, Starkey's defeat would have cheered Joe, but now he only felt despair as he rolled off Starkey and sat on the pier.

"He beat us," he said. "We'll never save Uncle Hugh now."

Frank sat next to him and searched for something to say, but there was nothing to be said. The antidote was gone, and they had lost.

"What am I bid for this?" said a woman's voice from below, and the Hardys' mouths fell open in astonishment as Charity came back up the ladder. In her hand was the vial. "Some fool threw it in the water. It's just lucky I happened to be down there to grab it."

"I'll take that now," said Frank. He reached out, but Charity snatched the vial from his grasp.

"Not so fast," she said. "I want the crown."

Frank shrugged and waved a thumb at Starkey. "It's in his pocket, but it won't do you any good. I don't think even you could get it to his customers, and there's no other way to make money from it."

"And I don't want to," Charity said. "I've got too much good taste to take part in spying." She motioned for them to move back. "That doesn't mean I plan to work with you. Away from him, or the vial goes overboard for real." They backed off. She stooped over Starkey and pulled his wallet from his pocket. "This ought to take care of my expenses. May I?"

"We need the antidote," Joe said. "Please."

"Tell you what. I'll trade you for the *real* crown. Where is it?"

"He had it," Frank said, nodding in Starkey's direction. "We don't know where it is."

Charity shrugged. "Too bad."

"Please," Joe pleaded. "You like scaring people, but I don't think you're a killer. There's a dying man in that warehouse, and what you hold in your hand is the only thing that can save his life. You've got to help."

"You're not conning me, are you?" she said. For a moment she seemed to soften. "Can I have the boat? I don't want to be around when Kwan and Tony find out I can't pay them."

THE HARDY BOYS CASEFILES

"Take anything you want," Joe said. "Just give us the vial."

Charity stepped forward and pressed the vial into Joe's hand. As she brushed by him, she kissed him lightly on the cheek and whispered in his ear, "If you ever need a partner in crime . . ."

Joe blushed. "I'll let you know," he said as she climbed in the boat and sped off across San Francisco Bay.

The next morning Frank and Joe entered the San Francisco offices of Transmutual Indemnity. Though it was still early, a team of government agents was clearing out the files and removing the furniture. The offices were being closed down, as was Espionage Resources. All that remained was for their uncle Hugh to clear out Starkey's private safe.

"Come in here, boys," he called from the inner office. He looked healthy again, though his hands still twitched and would until he was fully recovered from the poison. "I figured you'd want to be in on this. You did good work last night."

"Thanks," Frank said. "We're just glad you're okay."

"Thanks to you. That was some stunt you pulled, dragging in a street gang for a rumble. Just the sort of thinking we like to see in the business. Sure you don't want a job?"

Frank and Joe both shook their heads. Joe

asked, "You're not going to tell our mom and dad about all this, are you?"

"You know I can't, Joe. This is a top-security operation. Strictly hush-hush stuff." His uncle flashed him a conspiratorial wink. "So you'd better not tell them, either."

"You can count on that," Joe said. "What's going to happen to Starkey?" he asked.

At the sound of Starkey's name, Hugh became grim. "I'm not sure. If I had gotten his confession on tape, his fate would be a lot more certain. As it is, we may have to settle for shutting down his operation."

"Speaking of which, in all the excitement last night, I forgot to give this back to you," Joe said. He pulled his hand from his pocket and opened it to reveal his uncle's tiny tape recorder. "If the built-in microphone is any good, you should find it quite interesting. I had it on the whole time Starkey was taunting us last night."

Hugh Hunt's eyes brightened. "Joe, you're beautiful. Between that and his files, we've got enough to put Starkey away for a long time. You'll never guess who he was selling to."

"I thought it was the Russians," Frank said. "Or the Chinese."

"Not according to his records," his uncle revealed. "His clients were electronics manufacturers in Japan, South Korea, Hong Kong, and Malaysia. We develop the technology, they steal it, manufacture it cheaply, and sell the products here at prices we can't match. A neat little racket."

They moved across the room to a framed Rembrandt print, and Hugh moved it aside. A safe was imbedded in the wall behind it. "Starkey slipped up a little during questioning and told us where the art he stole was. We'll have the *real* crown back as soon as I get this wall safe open."

He spun the dial on the safe to the right, then to the left, then to the right again. "My hands are still a little shaky," he said. "Would one of you like to do the honors?"

Joe stepped forward and pressed down the safe handle. Dreaming of riches, he pulled open the door and stared inside.

He began to laugh.

"What's so funny?" Frank asked. He pushed past his brother and reached into the safe. The only contents were Starkey's wallet and a printed card.

"It's for us," Joe said. He took the card from Frank and held it up for his uncle to read:

BETTER LUCK NEXT TIME
LOVE AND KISSES,
CHARITY

"The woman?" Hugh asked.

"You got it," Joe said. With reluctant admiration, he sighed. "She pulled one last fast one on us. I hope we never run into her again."

But he had the feeling they would.

Be sure to read
all the books in the
Hardy Boys Casefiles Series:

CHILDREN'S ROOM

DATE DUE

DEC 1 8 1996			